P9-CEB-254

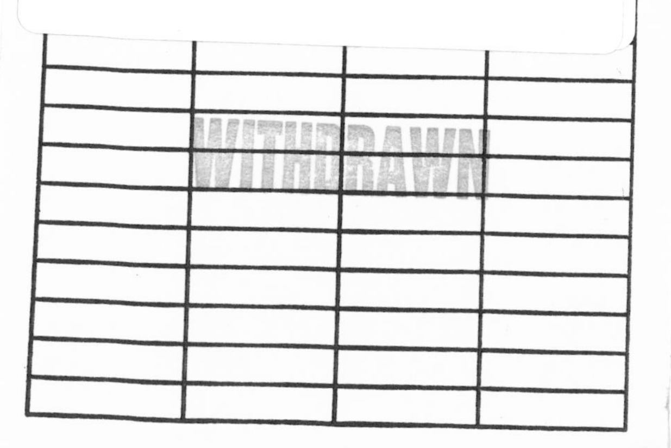
WITHDRAWN

WILL OF STEEL

Center Point
Large Print

Also by Diana Palmer
and available from Center Point Large Print:

Winter Roses
Iron Cowboy
Heart of Stone
Diamond in the Rough
The Maverick
Noelle

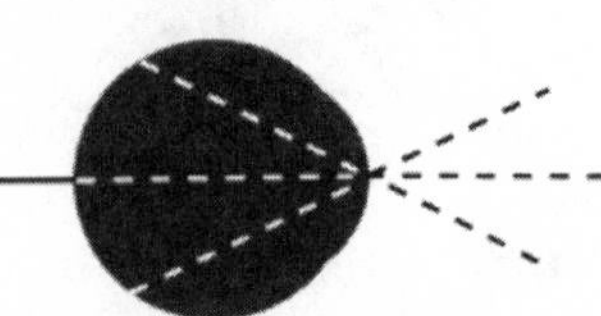

WILL OF STEEL

DIANA PALMER

CENTER POINT PUBLISHING
THORNDIKE, MAINE

This Center Point Large Print edition
is published in the year 2011 by arrangement with
Harlequin Books S.A.

The text of this Large Print edition is unabridged.
In other aspects, this book may vary
from the original edition.
Printed in the United States of America
on permanent paper.
Set in 16-point Times New Roman type.

ISBN: 978-1-60285-947-0

Library of Congress Cataloging-in-Publication Data

Palmer, Diana.
Will of steel / Diana Palmer. — Center Point large print ed.
p. cm.
ISBN 978-1-60285-947-0 (library binding : alk. paper)
1. Large type books. I. Title.
PS3566.A513W53 2011
813′.54—dc22

2010040909

Dear Reader,

Will of Steel started out to be a different sort of book altogether, a comedy about a young girl and a police chief who came together because of their respective uncles' wills. But that isn't how it turned out, as you will discover.

Authors know that characters tend to take on lives of their own once they are created. You can have a pattern for a book, but the hero and heroine can revise it to their own liking. No, I'm not certifiable: this is actually how the creative process works. So I plot the book, and the characters write it their own way.

Rourke was in *Tough to Tame* and *Dangerous*, and he popped up again in this book, with a bit more background. I didn't invite him, he just came along for the ride. He's one of those men I can't get rid of. Cash Grier was another. He'll get a book of his own down the line, I guess.

Thanks for your support and your kindness, and all the prayers and hugs. I am doing well, although I'm a little less mobile than I used to be. Chronic illness forces changes, not many of them welcome. I am grateful to have loyal fans and laptop computers and a thoughtful husband and understanding family. Those are blessings worth rubies in this world. The most beautiful ruby is my granddaughter, Selena, but I won't go on about that, although I could!

Much love to all of you, and thanks again for staying around and reading my books. You're the reason I can't stop writing them.

Love,

Diana Palmer

To the readers, all of you, many of whom are my friends on my Facebook page. You make this job wonderful and worthwhile. Thank you for your kindness and your support and your affection through all the long years. I am still your biggest fan.

WILL OF STEEL

Chapter 1

He never liked coming here. The stupid calf followed him around, everywhere he went. He couldn't get the animal to leave him alone. Once, he'd whacked the calf with a soft fir tree branch, but that had led to repercussions. Its owner had a lot to say about animal cruelty and quoted the law to him. He didn't need her to quote the law. He was, after all, the chief of police in the small Montana town where they both lived.

Technically, of course, this wasn't town. It was about two miles outside the Medicine Ridge city limits. A small ranch in Hollister, Montana, that included two clear, cold trout streams and half a mountain. Her uncle and his uncle had owned it jointly during their lifetimes. The two of them, best friends forever, had recently died, his uncle from a heart attack and hers, about a month later, in an airplane crash en route to a cattleman's convention. The property was set to go up on the auction block, and a California real estate developer was skulking in the wings, waiting to put in the winning bid. He was going to build a rich man's resort here, banking on those pure trout streams to bring in the business.

If Hollister Police Chief Theodore Graves had his way, the man would never set foot on the property. She felt that way, too. But the wily old men had placed a clause in both their wills pertaining to ownership of the land in question. The clause in her uncle's will had been a source of shock to Graves and the girl when the amused attorney read it out to them. It had provoked a war of words every time he walked in the door.

"I'm not marrying you," Jillian Sanders told him firmly the minute he stepped on the porch. "I don't care if I have to live in the barn with Sammy."

Sammy was the calf.

He looked down at her from his far superior height with faint arrogance. "No problem. I don't think the grammar school would give you a hall pass to marry me anyway."

Her pert nose wrinkled. "Well, you'd have to get permission from the old folks' home, and I'll bet you wouldn't get it, either!"

It was a standing joke. He was thirty-one to her almost twenty-one. They were completely mismatched. She was small and blonde and blue-eyed, he was tall and dark and black-eyed. He liked guns and working on his old truck when he wasn't performing his duties as chief of police in the small Montana community where they lived. She liked making up recipes for new sweets and he couldn't stand anything sweet except pound cake. She also hated guns and noise.

"If you don't marry me, Sammy will be featured on the menu in the local café, and you'll have to live in the woods in a cave," he pointed out.

That didn't help her disposition. She glared at him. It wasn't her fault that she had no family left alive. Her parents had died not long after she was born of an influenza outbreak. Her uncle had taken her in and raised her, but he was not in good health and had heart problems. Jillian had taken care of him as long as he was alive, fussing over his diet and trying to concoct special dishes to make him comfortable. But he'd died not of ill health, but in a light airplane crash on his way to a cattle convention. He didn't keep many cattle anymore, but he'd loved seeing friends at the conferences, and he loved to attend them. She missed him. It was lonely on the ranch. Of course, if she had to marry Rambo, here, it would be less lonely.

She glared at him, as if everything bad in her life could be laid at his door. "I'd almost rather live in the cave. I hate guns!" she added vehemently, noting the one he wore, old-fashioned style, on his hip in a holster. "You could blow a hole through a concrete wall with that thing!"

"Probably," he agreed.

"Why can't you carry something small, like your officers do?"

"I like to make an impression," he returned, tongue-in-cheek.

It took her a minute to get the insinuation. She glared at him even more.

He sighed. "I haven't had lunch," he said, and managed to look as if he were starving.

"There's a good café right downtown."

"Which will be closing soon because they can't get a cook," he said with disgust. "Damnedest thing, we live in a town where every woman cooks, but nobody wants to do it for the public. I guess I'll starve. I burn water."

It was the truth. He lived on takeout from the local café and frozen dinners. He glowered at her. "I guess marrying you would save my life. At least you can cook."

She gave him a smug look. "Yes, I can. And the local café isn't closing. They hired a cook just this morning."

"They did?" he exclaimed. "Who did they get?"

She averted her eyes. "I didn't catch her name, but they say she's talented. So you won't starve, I guess."

"Yes, but that doesn't help our situation here," he pointed out. His sensual lips made a thin line. "I don't want to get married."

"Neither do I," she shot back. "I've hardly even dated anybody!"

His eyebrows went up. "You're twenty years old. Almost twenty-one."

"Yes, and my uncle was suspicious of every man who came near me," she returned. "He made it impossible for me to leave the house."

His black eyes twinkled. "As I recall, you did escape once."

She turned scarlet. Yes, she had, with an auditor

who'd come to do the books for a local lawyer's office. The man, much older than her and more sophisticated, had charmed her. She'd trusted him, just as she'd trusted another man two years earlier. The auditor had taken her back to his motel room to get something he forgot. Or so he'd told her. Actually he'd locked the door and proceeded to try to remove her clothes. He was very nice about it, he was just insistent.

But he didn't know that Jillian had emotional scars already from a man trying to force her. She'd been so afraid. She'd really liked the man, trusted him. Uncle John hadn't. He always felt guilty about what she'd been through because of his hired man. She was underage, and he told her to stay away from the man.

But she'd had stars in her eyes because the man had flirted with her when she'd gone with Uncle John to see his attorney about a land deal. She'd thought he was different, nothing like Uncle John's hired man who had turned nasty.

He'd talked to her on the phone several times and persuaded her to go out with him. Infatuated, she sneaked out when Uncle John went to bed. But she landed herself in very hot water when the man got overly amorous. She'd managed to get her cell phone out and punched in 911. The result had been . . . unforgettable.

"They did get the door fixed, I believe . . . ?" she said, letting her voice trail off.

He glared at her. "It was locked."

"There's such a thing as keys," she pointed out.

"While I was finding one, you'd have been . . ."

She flushed again. She moved uncomfortably. "Yes, well, I did thank you. At the time."

"And a traveling mathematician learned the dangers of trying to seduce teenagers in my town."

She couldn't really argue. She'd been sixteen at the time, and Theodore's quick reaction had saved her honor. The auditor hadn't known her real age. She knew he'd never have asked her out if he had any idea she was under legal age. He'd been the only man she had a real interest in, for her whole life. He'd quit the firm he worked for, so he never had to come back to Hollister. She felt bad about it. The whole fiasco was her own fault.

The sad thing was that it wasn't her first scary episode with an older man. The first, at fifteen, had scarred her. She'd thought that she could trust a man again because she was crazy about the auditor. But the auditor became the icing on the cake of her withdrawal from the world of dating for good. She'd really liked him, trusted him, had been infatuated with him. He wasn't even a bad man, not like that other one . . .

"The judge did let him go with a severe reprimand about making sure of a girl's age and not trying to persuade her into an illegal act. But he could have gone to prison, and it would have been my fault," she recalled. She didn't mention the man who had gone to prison for assaulting her. Ted didn't know about that and she wasn't going to tell him.

"Don't look to me to have any sympathy for him," he said tersely. "Even if you'd been of legal age, he had no right to try to coerce you."

"Point taken."

"Your uncle should have let you get out more," he said reluctantly.

"I never understood why he kept me so close to home," she replied thoughtfully. She knew it wasn't all because of her bad experience.

His black eyes twinkled. "Oh, that's easy. He was saving you for me."

She gaped at him.

He chuckled. "He didn't actually say so, but you must have realized from his will that he'd planned a future for us for some time."

A lot of things were just becoming clear. She was speechless, for once.

He grinned. "He grew you in a hothouse just for me, little orchid," he teased.

"Obviously your uncle never did the same for me," she said scathingly.

He shrugged, and his eyes twinkled even more. "One of us has to know what to do when the time comes," he pointed out.

She flushed. "I think we could work it out without diagrams."

He leaned closer. "Want me to look it up and see if I can find some for you?"

"I'm not marrying you!" she yelled.

He shrugged. "Suit yourself. Maybe you can put up some curtains and lay a few rugs and the cave will be more comfortable." He glanced out the window. "Poor Sammy," he added sadly. "His future is less, shall we say, palatable."

"For the last time, Sammy is not a bull, he's a cow. She's a cow," she faltered.

"Sammy is a bull's name."

"She looked like a Sammy," she said stubbornly. "When she's grown, she'll give milk."

"Only when she's calving."

"Like you know," she shot back.

"I belong to the cattleman's association," he reminded her. "They tell us stuff like that."

"I belong to it, too, and no, they don't, you learn it from raising cattle!"

He tugged his wide-brimmed hat over his eyes. "It's useless, arguing with a blond fence post. I'm going back to work."

"Don't shoot anybody."

"I've never shot anybody."

"Ha!" she burst out. "What about that bank robber?"

"Oh. Him. Well, he shot at me first."

"Stupid of him."

He grinned. "That's just what he said, when I visited him in the hospital. He missed. I didn't.

And he got sentenced for assault on a police officer as well as the bank heist."

She frowned. "He swore he'd make you pay for that. What if he gets out?"

"Ten to twenty, and he's got priors," he told her. "I'll be in a nursing home for real by the time he gets out."

She glowered up at him. "People are always getting out of jail on technicalities. All he needs is a good lawyer."

"Good luck to him getting one on what he earns making license plates."

"The state provides attorneys for people who can't pay."

He gasped. "Thank you for telling me! I didn't know!"

"Why don't you go to work?" she asked, irritated.

"I've been trying to, but you won't stop flirting with me."

She gasped, but for real. "I am *not* flirting with you!"

He grinned. His black eyes were warm and sensuous as they met hers. "Yes, you are." He moved a step closer. "We could do an experiment. To see if we were chemically suited to each other."

She looked at him, puzzled, for a few seconds, until it dawned on her what he was suggesting. She moved back two steps, deliberately, and her high cheekbones flushed again. “I don’t want to do any experiments with you!”

He sighed. “Okay. But it’s going to be a very lonely marriage if you keep thinking that way, Jake.”

“Don’t call me Jake! My name is Jillian.”

He shrugged. “You’re a Jake.” He gave her a long look, taking in her ragged jeans and bulky gray sweatshirt and boots with curled-up toes from use. Her long blond hair was pinned up firmly into a topknot, and she wore no makeup. “Tomboy,” he added accusingly.

She averted her eyes. There were reasons she didn’t accentuate her feminine attributes, and she didn’t want to discuss the past with him. It wasn’t the sort of thing she felt comfortable talking about with anyone. It made Uncle John look bad, and he was dead. He’d cried about his lack of judgment in hiring Davy Harris. But it was too late by then.

Ted was getting some sort of vibrations from her. She was keeping something from him. He didn’t know what, but he was almost certain of it.

His teasing manner went into eclipse. He became a policeman again. “Is there something you want to talk to me about, Jake?” he asked in the soft tone he used with children.

She wouldn’t meet his eyes. “It wouldn’t help.”

“It might.”

She grimaced. "I don't know you well enough to tell you some things."

"If you marry me, you will."

"We've had this discussion," she pointed out.

"Poor Sammy."

"Stop that!" she muttered. "I'll find her a home. I could always ask John Callister if he and his wife, Sassy, would let her live with them."

"On their ranch where they raise purebred cattle."

"Sammy has purebred bloodlines on both sides," she muttered. "Her mother was a purebred Hereford cow and her father was a purebred Angus bull."

"And Sammy is a 'black baldy,'" he agreed, giving it the hybrid name. "But that doesn't make her a purebred cow."

"Semantics!" she shot back.

He grinned. "There you go, throwing those one-dollar words at me again."

"Don't pretend to be dumb, if you please. I happen to know that you got a degree in physics during your stint with the army."

He raised both thick black eyebrows. "Should I be flattered?"

"Why?"

"That you take an interest in my background."

"Everybody knows. It isn't just me."

He shrugged.

"Why are you a small-town police chief, with that sort of education?" she asked suddenly.

"Because I don't have the temperament for scientific research," he said simply. "Besides, you don't get to play with guns in a laboratory."

"I hate guns."

"You said."

"I really mean it." She shivered dramatically. "You could shoot somebody by accident. Didn't one of your patrolmen drop his pistol in a grocery store and it went off?"

He looked grim. "Yes, he did. He was off duty and carrying his little .32 wheel gun in his pants pocket. He reached for change and it fell out and discharged." He pursed his lips. "A mistake I can guarantee he will never make again."

"So his wife said. You are one mean man when you lose your temper, do you know that?"

"The pistol discharged into a display of cans, fortunately for him, and we only had to pay damages to the store. But it could have discharged into a child, or a grown-up, with tragic results. There are reasons why they make holsters for guns."

She looked at his pointedly. "That one sure is fancy," she noted, indicating the scrollwork on the soft tan leather. It also sported silver conchos and fringe.

"My cousin made it for me."

"Tanika?" she asked, because she knew his cousin, a full-blooded Cheyenne who lived down near Hardin.

"Yes." He smiled. "She thinks practical gear should have beauty."

"She's very gifted." She smiled. "She makes some gorgeous *parfleche* bags. I've seen them at the trading post in Hardin, near the Little Bighorn Battlefield." They were rawhide bags with beaded trim and fringe, incredibly beautiful and useful for transporting items in the old days for native people.

"Thank you," he said abruptly.

She lifted her eyebrows. "For what?"

"For not calling it the Custer Battlefield."

A lot of people did. He had nothing against Custer, but his ancestry was Cheyenne. He had relatives who had died in the Little Bighorn Battle and, later, at Wounded Knee. Custer was a sore spot with him. Some tourists didn't seem to realize that Native Americans considered that people other than Custer's troops were killed in the battle.

She smiled. "I think I had a Sioux ancestor."

"You look like it," he drawled, noting her fair coloring.

"My cousin Rabby is half and half, and he has blond hair and gray eyes," she reminded him.

"I guess so." He checked the big watch on his wrist. "I've got to be in court for a preliminary hearing. Better go."

"I'm baking a pound cake."

He hesitated. "Is that an invitation?"

"You did say you were starving."

“Yes, but you can’t live on cake.”

“So I’ll fry a steak and some potatoes to go with it.”

His lips pulled up into a smile. “Sounds nice. What time?”

“About six? Barring bank robberies and insurgent attacks, of course.”

“I’m sure we won’t have one today.” He considered her invitation. “The Callisters brought me a flute back from Cancún when they went on their honeymoon. I could bring it and serenade you.”

She flushed a little. The flute and its connection with courting in the Native American world was quite well-known. “That would be nice.”

“It would?”

“I thought you were leaving.” She didn’t quite trust that smile.

“I guess I am. About six?”

“Yes.”

“I’ll see you then.” He paused with his hand on the doorknob. “Should I wear my tuxedo?”

“It’s just steak.”

“No dancing afterward?” he asked, disappointed.

“Not unless you want to build a bonfire outside and dance around it.” She frowned. “I think I know one or two steps from the women’s dances.”

He glared at her. “Ballroom dancing isn’t done around campfires.”

"You can do ballroom dances?" she asked, impressed.
"Of course I can."
"Waltz, polka . . . ?"
"Tango," he said stiffly.
Her eyes twinkled. "Tango? Really?"
"Really. One of my friends in the service learned it down in Argentina. He taught me."
"What an image that brings to mind—" she began, tongue-in-cheek.
"He didn't teach me by dancing with me!" he shot back. "He danced with a girl."
"Well, I should hope so," she agreed.
"I'm leaving."
"You already said."
"This time, I mean it." He walked out.
"Six!" she called after him.
He threw up a hand. He didn't look back.

Jillian closed the door and leaned back against it. She was a little apprehensive, but after all, she had to marry somebody. She knew Theodore Graves better than she knew any other men. And, despite their quarreling, they got along fairly well.

The alternative was to let some corporation build a holiday resort here in Hollister, and it would be a disaster for local ranching. Resorts brought in all sorts of amusement, plus hotels and gas stations and businesses. It would be a boon for the economy, but Hollister would lose its rural, small-town appeal. It wasn't something Jillian would enjoy and she was certain that other people would feel the same. She loved the forests with their tall lodgepole pines, and the shallow, diamond-bright trout streams where she loved to fish when she had free time. Occasionally Theodore would bring over his spinning reel and join her. Then they'd work side by side, scaling and filleting fish and frying them, along with hush puppies, in a vat of hot oil. Her mouth watered, just thinking about it.

She wandered into the kitchen. She'd learned to cook from one of her uncle's rare girlfriends. It had delighted her. She might be a tomboy, but she had a natural affinity for flour and she could make bread from scratch. It amazed her how few people could. The feel of the dough, soft and smooth, was a gift to her fingertips when she kneaded and punched and worked it. The smell of fresh bread in the kitchen was a delight for the senses. She always had fresh homemade butter to go on it, which she purchased from an elderly widow just down the road. Theodore loved fresh bread. She was making a batch for tonight, to go with the pound cake.

She pulled out her bin of flour and got down some yeast from the shelf. It took a long time to make bread from scratch, but it was worth it.

She hadn't changed into anything fancy, although she did have on a new pair of blue jeans and a pink checked shirt that buttoned up. She also tucked a pink ribbon into her long blond hair, which she tidied into a bun on top of her head. She wasn't elegant, or beautiful, but she could at least look like a girl when she tried.

And he noticed the minute he walked in the door. He cocked his head and stared down at her with amusement.

"You're a girl," he said with mock surprise.

She glared up at him. "I'm a woman."

He pursed his lips. "Not yet."

She flushed. She tried for a comeback but she couldn't fumble one out of her flustered mind.

"Sorry," he said gently, and became serious when he noted her reaction to the teasing. "That wasn't fair. Especially since you went to all the trouble to make me fresh rolls." He lifted his head and sniffed appreciably.

"How did you know that?"

He tapped his nose. "I have a superlative sense of smell. Did I ever tell you about the time I tracked a wanted murderer by the way he smelled?" he added. "He was wearing some gosh-awful cheap cologne. I just followed the scent and walked up to him with my gun out. He'd spent a whole day covering his trail and stumbling over rocks to throw me off the track. He was so shocked when I walked into his camp that he just gave up without a fight."

"Did you tell him that his smell gave him away?" she asked, chuckling.

"No. I didn't want him to mention it to anybody when he went to jail. No need to give criminals a heads-up about something like that."

"Native Americans are great trackers," she commented.

He glowered down at her. "Anybody can be a good tracker. It comes from training, not ancestry."

"Well, aren't you touchy," she exclaimed.

He averted his eyes. He shrugged. "Banes has been at it again."

"You should assign him to school crossings. He hates that," she advised.

"No, he doesn't. His new girlfriend is a widow. She's got a little boy, and Banes has suddenly become his hero. He'd love to work the school crossing."

"Still, you could find some unpleasant duty to assign him. Didn't he say once that he hates being on traffic detail at ball games?"

He brightened. "You know, he did say that."

"See? An opportunity presents itself." She frowned. "Why are we looking for ways to punish him this time?"

"He brought in a new book on the Little Bighorn Battle and showed me where it said Crazy Horse wasn't in the fighting."

She gave him a droll look. "Oh, sure."

He grimaced. "Every so often, some writer who never saw a real Native American gets a bunch of hearsay evidence together and writes a book about how he's the only one who knows the true story of some famous battle. This guy also said that Custer was nuts and had a hand in the post trader scandal where traders were cheating the Sioux and Cheyenne."

"Nobody who reads extensively about Custer would believe he had a hand in something so dishonest," she scoffed. "He went to court and testified against President Ulysses S. Grant's own brother in that corruption trial, as I recall. Why would he take such a risk if he was personally involved in it?"

"My thoughts exactly," he said, "and I told Banes so."

"What did Banes say to that?"

"He quoted the author's extensive background in military history."

She gave him a suspicious look. "Yes? What sort of background?"

"He's an expert in the Napoleonic Wars."

"Great! What does that have to do with the campaign on the Greasy Grass?" she asked, which referred to the Lakota name for the battle.

"Not a damned thing," he muttered. "You can be brilliant in your own field of study, but it's another thing to do your research from a standing start and come to all the wrong conclusions. Banes said the guy used period newspapers and magazines for part of his research."

"The Lakota and Cheyenne, as I recall, didn't write about current events," she mused.

He chuckled. "No, they didn't have newspaper reporters back then. So it was all from the cavalry's point of view, or that of politicians. History is the story of mankind written by the victors."

"Truly."

He smiled. "You're pretty good on local history."

"That's because I'm related to people who helped make it."

"Me, too." He cocked his head. "I ought to take you down to Hardin and walk the battlefield with you sometime," he said.

Her eyes lit up. "I'd love that."

"So would I."

"There's a trading post," she recalled.

"They have some beautiful things there."

"Made by local talent," she agreed. She sighed. "I get so tired of so-called Native American art made in China. Nothing against the Chinese. I mean, they have aboriginal peoples, too. But if you're going to sell things that are supposed to be made by tribes in this country, why import them?"

"Beats me. Ask somebody better informed."

"You're a police chief," she pointed out. "There isn't supposed to be anybody better informed."

He grinned. "Thanks."

She curtsied.

He frowned. "Don't you own a dress?"

"Sure. It's in my closet." She pursed her lips. "I wore it to graduation."

"Spare me!"

"I guess I could buy a new one."

"I guess you could. I mean, if we're courting, it will look funny if you don't wear a dress."

"Why?"

He blinked. "You going to get married in blue jeans?"

"For the last time, I am not going to marry you."

He took off his wide-brimmed hat and laid it on the hall table. "We can argue about that later. Right now, we need to eat some of that nice, warm, fresh bread before it gets cold and butter won't melt on it. Shouldn't we?" he added with a grin.

She laughed. "I guess we should."

Chapter 2

The bread was as delicious as he'd imagined it would be. He closed his eyes, savoring the taste.

"You could cook, if you'd just try," she said.

"Not really. I can't measure stuff properly."

"I could teach you."

"Why do I need to learn how, when you do it so well already?" he asked reasonably.

"You live alone," she began.

He raised an eyebrow. "Not for long."

"For the tenth time today . . ."

"The California guy was in town today," he said grimly. "He came by the office to see me."

"He did?" She felt apprehensive.

He nodded as he bit into another slice of buttered bread with perfect white teeth. "He's already approached contractors for bids to build his housing project." He bit the words off as he was biting the bread.

"Oh."

Jet-black eyes pierced hers. "I told him about the clause in the will."

"What did he say?"

"That he'd heard you wouldn't marry me."

She grimaced.

"He was strutting around town like a tom turkey," he added. He finished the bread and sipped coffee. His eyes closed as he savored it.

"You make great coffee, Jake!" he exclaimed. "Most people wave the coffee over water. You could stand up a spoon in this."

"I like it strong, too," she agreed. She studied his hard, lean face. "I guess you live on it when you have cases that keep you out all night tracking. There have been two or three of those this month alone."

He nodded. "Our winter festival brings in people from all over the country. Some of them see the mining company's bankroll as a prime target."

"Not to mention the skeet-and-trap-shooting regional championships," she said. "I've heard that thieves actually follow the shooters around and get license plate numbers of cars whose owners have the expensive guns."

"They're targets, all right."

"Why would somebody pay five figures for a gun?" she wondered out loud.

He laughed. "You don't shoot in competition, so it's no use trying to explain it to you."

"You compete," she pointed out. "You don't have a gun that expensive and you're a triple-A shooter."

He shrugged. "It isn't that I wouldn't like to have one. But unless I take up bank robbing, I'm not likely to be able to afford one, either. The best I can do is borrow one for the big competitions."

Her eyes popped. "You know somebody who'll loan you a fifty-thousand-dollar shotgun?"

He laughed. "Well, actually, yes, I do. He's police chief of a small town down in Texas. He used to do shotgun competitions when he was younger, and he still has the hardware."

"And he loans you the gun."

"He isn't attached to it, like some owners are. Although, you'd never get him to loan his sniper kit," he chuckled.

"Excuse me?"

He leaned toward her. "He was a covert assassin in his shady past."

"Really?" She was excited by the news.

He frowned. "What do women find so fascinating about men who shoot people?"

She blinked. "It's not that."

"Then what is it?"

She hesitated, trying to put it into words. "Men who have been in battles have tested themselves in a way most people never have to," she began slowly. "They learn their own natures. They . . . I can't exactly express it . . ."

"They learn what they're made of, right where they live and breathe," he commented. "Under fire, you're always afraid. But you harness the fear and use it, attack when you'd rather run. You learn the meaning of courage. It isn't the absence of fear. It's fear management, at its best. You do your duty."

"Nicely said, Chief Graves," she said admiringly, and grinned.

"Well, I know a thing or two about being shot

at," he reminded her. "I was in the first wave in the second incursion in the Middle East. Then I became a police officer and then a police chief."

"You met the other police chief at one of those conventions, I'll bet," she commented.

"Actually I met him at the FBI academy during a training session on hostage negotiation," he corrected. "He was teaching it."

"My goodness. He can negotiate?"

"He did most of his negotiations with a gun before he was a Texas Ranger," he laughed.

"He was a Ranger, too?"

"Yes. And a cyber-crime expert for a Texas D.A., and a merc, and half a dozen other interesting things. He can also dance. He won a tango contest in Argentina, and that's saying something. Tango and Argentina go together like coffee and cream."

She propped her chin in her hands. "A man who can do the tango. It boggles the mind. I've only ever seen a couple of men do it in movies." She smiled. "Al Pacino in *Scent of a Woman* was my favorite."

He grinned. "Not the 'governator' in *True Lies*?"

She glared at him. "I'm sure he was doing his best."

He shook his head. "I watched Rudolph Valentino do it in an old silent film," he sighed. "Real style."

"It's a beautiful dance."

He gave her a long look. “There’s a new Latin dance club in Billings.”

“What?” she exclaimed with pure surprise.

“No kidding. A guy from New York moved out here to retire. He’d been in ballroom competition most of his life and he got bored. So he organized a dance band and opened up a dance club. People come up from Wyoming and across from the Dakotas just to hear the band and do the dances.” He toyed with his coffee cup. “Suppose you and I go up there and try it out? I can teach you the tango.”

Her heart skipped. It was the first time, despite all the banter, that he’d ever suggested taking her on a date.

He scowled when she hesitated.

“I’d love to,” she blurted out.

His face relaxed. He smiled again. “Okay. Saturday?”

She nodded. Her heart was racing. She felt breathless.

She was so young, he thought, looking at her. He hesitated.

“They don’t have grammar school on Saturdays,” she quipped, “so I won’t need an excuse from the principal to skip class.”

He burst out laughing. “Is that how I looked? Sorry.”

“I’m almost twenty-one,” she pointed out. “I know that seems young to you, but I’ve had a lot of responsibility. Uncle John could be a handful, and I was the only person taking care of him for most of my life."

"That's true. Responsibility matures people pretty quick."

"You'd know," she said softly, because he'd taken wonderful care of his grandmother and then the uncle who'd owned half this ranch.

He shrugged. "I don't think there's a choice about looking after people you love."

"Neither do I."

He gave her an appraising look. "You going to the club in blue jeans and a shirt?" he asked. "Because if you are, I plan to wear my uniform."

She raised both eyebrows.

"Or have you forgotten what happened the last time I wore my uniform to a social event?" he added.

She glowered at him.

"Is it my fault if people think of me as a target the minute they realize what I do for a living?" he asked.

"You didn't have to anoint him with punch."

"Sure I did. He was so hot under the collar about a speeding ticket my officer gave him that he needed instant cooling off."

She laughed. "Your patrolman is still telling that story."

"With some exaggerations he added to it," Theodore chuckled.

"It cured the guy of complaining to you."

"Yes, it did. But if I wear my uniform to a dance club where people drink, there's bound to be at least one guy who thinks I'm a target."

She sighed.

"And since you're with me, you'd be right in the thick of it." He pursed his lips. "You wouldn't like to be featured in a riot, would you?"

"Not in Billings, no," she agreed.

"Then you could wear a skirt, couldn't you?"

"I guess it wouldn't kill me," she said, but reluctantly.

He narrowed his eyes as he looked at her. There was some reason she didn't like dressing like a woman. He wished he could ask her about it, but she was obviously uncomfortable discussing personal issues with him. Maybe it was too soon. He did wonder if she still had scars from her encounter with the auditor.

He smiled gently. "Something demure," he added. "I won't expect you to look like a pole dancer, okay?"

She laughed. "Okay."

He loved the way she looked when she smiled. Her whole face took on a radiance that made her pretty. She didn't smile often. Well, neither did he. His job was a somber one, most of the time.

"I'll see you about six, then."

She nodded. She was wondering how she was

going to afford something new to wear to a fancy nightclub, but she would never have admitted it to him.

She ran into Sassy Callister in town while she was trying to find something presentable on the bargain table at the single women's clothing store.

"You're looking for a dress?" Sassy exclaimed. She'd known Jillian all her life, and she'd never seen her in anything except jeans and shirts. She even wore a pantsuit to church when she went.

Jillian glared at her. "I do have legs."

"That wasn't what I meant." She chuckled. "I gather Ted's taking you out on a real date, huh?"

Jillian went scarlet. "I never said . . . !"

"Oh, we all know about the will," Sassy replied easily. "It's sensible, for the two of you to get married and keep the ranch in the family. Nobody wants to see some fancy resort being set up here," she added, "with outsiders meddling in our local politics and throwing money around to get things the way they think they should be."

Jillian's eyes twinkled. "Imagine you complaining about the rich, when you just married one of the richest men in Montana."

"You know what I mean," Sassy laughed. "And I'll remind you that I didn't know he was rich when I accepted his proposal."

"A multimillionaire pretending to be a ranch foreman." Jillian shook her head. "It came as a shock to a lot of us when we found out who he really was."

"I assure you that it was more of a shock to me," came the amused reply. "I tried to back out of it, but he wouldn't let me. He said that money was an accessory, not a character trait. You should meet his brother and sister-in-law," she added with a grin. "Her parents were missionaries and her aunt is a nun. Oh, and her godfather is one of the most notorious ex-mercenaries who ever used a gun."

"My goodness!"

"But they're all very down-to-earth. They don't strut, is what I mean."

Jillian giggled. "I get it."

Sassy gave her a wise look. "You want something nice for that date, but you're strained to the gills trying to manage on what your uncle left you."

Jillian started to deny it, but she gave up. Sassy was too sweet to lie to. "Yes," she confessed. "I was working for old Mrs. Rogers at the florist shop. Then she died and the shop closed." She sighed. "Not many jobs going in a town this small. You'd know all about that," she added, because Sassy had worked for a feed store and was assaulted by her boss. Fortunately she was rescued by her soon-to-be husband and the perpetrator had been sent to jail. But it was the only job Sassy could get. Hollister was very small.

Sassy nodded. "I wouldn't want to live anyplace

else, though. Even if I had to commute back and forth to Billings to get a job." She laughed. "I considered that, but I didn't think my old truck would get me that far." Her eyes twinkled. "Chief Graves said that if he owned a piece of junk like I was driving, he'd be the first to agree to marry a man who could afford to replace it for me."

Jillian burst out laughing. "I can imagine what you said to that."

She laughed, too. "I just expressed the thought that he wouldn't marry John Callister for a truck." She cocked her head. "He really is a catch, you know. Theodore Graves is the stuff of legends around here. He's honest and kindhearted and a very mean man to make an enemy of. He'd take care of you."

"Well, he needs more taking care of than I do," came the droll reply. "At least I can cook."

"Didn't you apply for the cook's job at the restaurant?"

"I did. I got it, too, but you can't tell Theodore."

"I won't. But why can't I?"

Jillian sighed. "In case things don't work out, I want to have a means of supporting myself. He'll take it personally if he thinks I got a job before he even proposed."

"He's old-fashioned."

"Nothing wrong with that," Jillian replied with a smile.

"Of course not. It's just that some men have to be

hit over the head so they'll accept that modern women can have outside interests without giving up family. Come over here."

She took Jillian's arm and pulled her to one side. "Everything in here is a three-hundred-percent markup," she said under her breath. "I love Jessie, but she's overpriced. You're coming home with me. We're the same size and I've got a closet full of stuff you can wear. You can borrow anything you like. Heck, you can have what you like. I'll never wear all of it anyway."

Jillian flushed red and stammered, "No, I couldn't . . . !"

"You could and you're going to. Now come on!"

Jillian was transported to the Callister ranch in a Jaguar. She was so fascinated with it that she didn't hear half of what her friend was saying.

"Look at all these gadgets!" she exclaimed. "And this is real wood on the dash!"

"Yes," Sassy laughed. "I acted the same as you, the first time I rode in it. My old battered truck seemed so pitiful afterward."

"I like my old car. But this is amazing," she replied, touching the silky wood.

"I know."

"It's so nice of you to do this," Jillian replied. "Theodore wanted me to wear a skirt. I don't even own one."

Sassy looked at her briefly. “You should tell him, Jilly.”

She flushed and averted her eyes. “Nobody knows but you and your mother. And I know you won’t say anything.”

“Not unless you said I could,” Sassy replied. “But it could cause you some problems later on. Especially after you’re married.”

Jillian clenched her teeth. “I’ll cross that bridge if I come to it. I may not marry Theodore. We may be able to find a way to break the will.”

“One, maybe. Two, never.”

That was true. Both old men had left ironclad wills with clauses about the disposition of the property if Theodore and Jillian refused to get married.

“The old buzzards!” Jillian burst out. “Why did they have to complicate things like that? Theodore and I could have found a way to deal with the problem on our own!”

“I don’t know. Neither of you is well-off, and that California developer has tons of money. I’ll bet he’s already trying to find a way to get to one of you about buying the ranch outright once you inherit.”

“He’ll never get it,” she said stubbornly.

Sassy was going to comment that rich people with intent sometimes knew shady ways to make people do what they wanted them to. But the developer wasn’t local and he didn’t have any information he could use to blackmail either

Theodore or Jillian, so he probably couldn't force them to sell to him. He'd just sit and wait and hope they couldn't afford to keep it. Fat chance, Sassy thought solemly. She and John would bail them out if they had to. No way was some out-of-state fat cat taking over Jillian's land. Not after all she'd gone through in her young life.

Maybe it was a good thing Theodore didn't know everything about his future potential wife. But Jillian was setting herself up for some real heartbreak if she didn't level with him. After all, he was in law enforcement. He could dig into court records and find things that most people didn't have access to. He hadn't been in town when Jillian faced her problems, he'd been away at the FBI Academy on a training mission. And since only Sassy and her mother, Mrs. Peale, had been involved, nobody else except the prosecuting attorney and the judge and the public defender had knowledge about the case. Not that any of them would disclose it.

She was probably worrying unnecessarily. She smiled at Jillian. "You are right. He'll never get the ranch," she agreed.

They pulled up at the house. It had been given a makeover and it looked glorious.

"You've done a lot of work on this place," Jillian commented. "I remember what it looked like before."

"So do I. John wanted to go totally green here, so we have solar power and wind generators. And the electricity in the barn runs on methane from the cattle refuse."

"It's just fantastic," Jillian commented. "Expensive, too, I'll bet."

"That's true, but the initial capital outlay was the highest. It will pay for itself over the years."

"And you'll have lower utility bills than the rest of us," Jillian sighed, thinking about her upcoming one. It had been a colder than usual winter. Heating oil was expensive.

"Stop worrying," Sassy told her. "Things work out."

"You think?"

They walked down the hall toward the master bedroom. "How's your mother?" Jillian asked.

"Doing great. She got glowing reports from her last checkup," Sassy said. The cancer had been contained and her mother hadn't had a recurrence, thanks to John's interference at a critical time. "She always asks about you."

"Your mother is the nicest person I know, next to you. How about Selene?"

The little girl was one Mrs. Peale had adopted. She was in grammar school, very intelligent and with definite goals. "She's reading books about the Air Force," Sassy laughed. "She wants to be a fighter pilot."

"Wow!"

"That's what we said, but she's very focused. She's good at math and science, too. We think she may end up being an engineer."

"She's smart."

"Very."

Sassy opened the closet and started pulling out dresses and skirts and blouses in every color under the sun.

Jillian just stared at them, stunned. "I've never seen so many clothes outside a department store," she stammered.

Sassy chuckled. "Neither did I before I married John. He spoils me rotten. Every birthday and holiday I get presents from him. Pick something out."

"You must have favorites that you don't want to loan," Jillian began.

"I do. That's why they're still in the closet," she said with a grin.

"Oh."

Sassy was eyeing her and then the clothes on the bed. "How about this?" She picked up a patterned blue skirt, very long and silky, with a pale blue silk blouse that had puffy sleeves and a rounded neckline. It looked demure, but it was a witchy ensemble. "Try that on. Let's see how it looks."

Jillian's hands fumbled. She'd never put on something so expensive. It fit her like a glove, and it felt good to move in, as so many clothes didn't. She remarked on that.

"Most clothes on the rack aren't constructed to fit exactly, and the less expensive they are, the worse the fit," Sassy said. "I know, because I bought clothes off the sales rack all my life before I married. I was shocked to find that expensive clothes actually fit. And when they do, they make you look better. You can see for yourself."

Jillian did. Glancing in the mirror, she was shocked to find that the skirt put less emphasis on her full hips and more on her narrow waist. The blouse, on the other hand, made her small breasts look just a little bigger.

"Now, with your hair actually down and curled, instead of screwed up into that bun," Sassy continued, pulling out hairpins as she went and reaching for a brush, "you'll look so different that Ted may not even recognize you. What a difference!"

It was. With her long blond hair curling around her shoulders, she looked really pretty.

"Is that me?" she asked, shocked.

Sassy grinned. "Sure is."

She turned to her friend, fighting tears. "It's so nice of you," she began.

Sassy hugged her. "Friends look out for each other."

They hadn't been close friends, because Sassy's home problems had made that impossible before her marriage. But they were growing closer now. It was nice to have someone she could talk to.

She drew away and wiped at her eyes. "Sorry. Didn't mean to do that."

"You're a nice person, Jilly," Sassy told her gently. "You'd do the same for me in a heartbeat, if our situations were reversed, and you know it."

"I certainly would."

"I've got some curlers. Let's put up your hair in them and then we can snap beans."

"You've got beans in the middle of winter?" Jillian exclaimed.

"From the organic food market," she laughed. "I have them shipped in. You can take some home and plant up. Ted might like beans and ham hocks."

"Even if he didn't, I sure would. I'll bet it's your own pork."

"It is. We like organic all the way. Put your jeans back on and we'll wash your hair and set it. It's thin enough that it can dry while we work."

And it did. They took the curlers out a couple of hours later. Jillian was surprised at the difference a few curls made in her appearance.

"Makeup next," Sassy told her, grinning. "This is fun!"

"Fun and educational," Jillian said, still reeling. "How did you learn all this?"

"From my mother-in-law. She goes to spas and beauty parlors all the time. She's still gorgeous, even though she's gaining in years. Sit down."

Sassy put her in front of a fluorescent-lit mirror and proceeded to experiment with different shades of lipstick and eye shadow. Jillian felt as spoiled as if she'd been to an exclusive department store, and she said so.

"I'm still learning," Sassy assured her. "But it's fun, isn't it?"

"The most fun I've had in a long time, and thank you. Theodore is going to be shocked when he shows up Saturday!" she predicted.

Shocked was an understatement. Jillian in a blue ensemble, with her long hair soft and curling around her shoulders, with demure makeup, was a revelation to a man who'd only ever seen her without makeup in ragged jeans and sweatshirts or, worse, baggy T-shirts. Dressed up, in clothes that fit her perfectly, she was actually pretty.

"You can close your mouth, Theodore," she teased, delighted at his response.

He did. He shook his head. "You look nice," he said. It was an understatement, compared to what he was thinking. Jillian was a knockout. He frowned as he thought how her new look might go down in town. There were a couple of younger men, nice-looking ones with wealthy backgrounds, who might also find the new Jillian a hot item. He might have competition for her that he couldn't handle.

Jillian, watching his expressions change, was

suddenly insecure. He was scowling as if he didn't actually approve of how she looked.

"It isn't too revealing, is it?" she worried.

He cleared his throat. "Jake, you're covered from stem to stern, except for the hollow of your throat, and your arms," he said. "What do you think is revealing?"

"You looked . . . well, you looked . . ."

"I looked like a man who's considering the fight ahead."

"Excuse me?"

He moved a step closer and looked down at her with pure appreciation. "You really don't know what a knockout you are, all dressed up?"

Her breath caught in her throat. "Me?"

His big hands framed her face and brought it up to his dancing black eyes. "You." He rubbed his nose against hers. "You know, I really wonder if you taste as good as you look. This is as good a time as any to find out."

He bent his head as he spoke and, for the first time in their relationship, he kissed her, right on the mouth. Hard.

Whatever he expected her reaction to be, the reality of it came as a shock . . .

Chapter 3

Jillian jerked back away from him as if he'd offended her, flushing to the roots of her hair. She stared at him with helpless misery, waiting for the explosion. The auditor had cursed a blue streak, called her names, swore that he'd tell every boy he knew that she was a hopeless little icicle.

But Theodore didn't do that. In fact, he smiled, very gently.

She bit her lower lip. She wanted to tell him. She couldn't. The pain was almost physical.

He took her flushed face in his big hands and bent and kissed her gently on the forehead, then on her eyelids, closing them.

"We all have our own secret pain, Jake," he whispered. "One day you'll want to tell me, and I'll listen." He lifted his head. "For the time being, we'll be best buddies, except that you're wearing a skirt," he added, tongue-in-cheek. "I have to confess that very few of my buddies have used a women's restroom."

It took her a minute, then she burst out laughing.

"That's better," he said, and grinned. He cocked his head and gave her a very male appraisal. "You really do look nice." He pursed his lips as he contemplated the ensemble and its probable cost.

"They're loaners," she blurted out.

His black eyes sparkled with unholy glee. “Loaners?”

She nodded. “Sassy Callister.”

“I see.”

She grinned. “She said that she had a whole closet of stuff she never wore. I didn’t want to, but she sort of bulldozed me into it. She’s a lot like her new husband.”

“He wears petticoats?” he asked outrageously.

She glared at him. “Women don’t wear petticoats or hoop skirts these days, Theodore.”

“Sorry. Wrong era.”

She grinned. “Talk about living in the dark ages!”

He shrugged. “I was raised by my grandmother and my uncle. They weren’t forthcoming about women’s intimate apparel.”

“Well, I guess not!”

“Your uncle John was the same sort of throwback,” he remarked.

“So we both come by it honestly, I suppose.” She noted his immaculate dark suit and the spotless white shirt and blue patterned tie he was wearing with it. “You look nice, too.”

“I bought the suit to wear to John Callister’s wedding,” he replied. “I don’t often have the occasion to dress up.”

“Me, neither,” she sighed.

“I guess we could go a few places together,” he commented. “I like to hunt and fish.”

“I do not like guns,” she said flatly.

“Well, in my profession, they’re sort of a necessity, Jake,” he commented.

“I suppose so. Sorry.”

“No problem. You used to like fishing.”

“It’s been a while since I dipped a poor, helpless worm into the water.”

He chuckled. “Everything in life has a purpose. A worm’s is to help people catch delicious fish.”

“The worm might not share your point of view.”

“I’ll ask, the next time I see one.”

She laughed, and her whole face changed. She felt better than she had in ages. Theodore didn’t think she was a lost cause. He wasn’t even angry that she’d gone cold at his kiss. Maybe, she thought, just maybe, there was still hope for her.

His black eyes were kind. “I’m glad you aren’t wearing high heels,” he commented.

“Why?”

He glanced down at his big feet in soft black leather boots. “Well, these aren’t as tough as the boots I wear on the job. I’d hate to have holes in them from spiked heels, when you step on my feet on the dance floor.”

“I will not step on your feet,” she said with mock indignation. She grinned. “I might trip over them and land in a flowerpot, of course.”

“I heard about that,” he replied, chuckling. “Poor old Harris Twain. I’ll bet he’ll never stick his legs out into the walkway of a restaurant again. He said you were pretty liberally covered with potting soil. You went in headfirst, I believe . . . ?"

She sighed. "Most people have talents. Mine is lack of coordination. I can trip over my own feet, much less someone else's."

He wondered about that clumsiness. She was very capable, in her own way, but she often fell. He frowned.

"Now, see, you're thinking that I'm a klutz, and you're absolutely right."

"I was wondering more about your balance," he said. "Do you have inner ear problems?"

She blinked. "What do my ears have to do with that?"

"A lot. If you have an inner ear disturbance, it can affect balance."

"And where did you get your medical training?" she queried.

"I spend some time in emergency rooms, with victims and perps alike. I learn a lot about medical problems that way."

"I forgot."

He shrugged. "It goes with the job."

"I don't have earaches," she said, and averted her eyes. "Shouldn't we get going?"

She was hiding something. A lot, maybe. He let it go. "I guess we should."

"A Latin dance club in Billings." She grinned. "How exotic!"

"The owner's even more exotic. You'll like

him." He leaned closer. "He was a gun runner in his wild youth."

"Wow!"

"I thought you'd be impressed. So was I."

"You have an interesting collection of strange people in your life," she commented on the way to his truck.

"Goes with the—"

"Job. I guess." She grinned when she saw the truck. "Washed and waxed it, huh?" she teased.

"Well, you can't take a nice woman to a dance in a dirty truck," he stated.

"I wouldn't have minded."

He turned to her at the passenger side of the truck and looked down at her solemnly in the light from the security lamp on a pole nearby. His face was somber. "No, you wouldn't. You don't look at bank accounts to judge friendships. It's one of a lot of things I like about you. I dated a woman attorney once, who came here to try a case for a client in district court. When she saw the truck, the old one I had several years ago, she actually backed out of the date. She said she didn't want any important people in the community to see her riding around in a piece of junk."

She gasped. "No! How awful for you!"

His high cheekbones had a faint flush. Her indignation made him feel warm inside. "Something you'd never have said to me, as blunt as you are. It turned me off women for a while. Not that I even liked her. But it hurt my pride."

"As if a vehicle was any standard to base a character assessment on," she huffed.

He smiled tenderly. "Small-town police chiefs don't usually drive Jaguars. Although this guy I know in Texas does. But he made his money as a merc, not in law enforcement."

"I like you just the way you are," she told him quietly. "And it wouldn't matter to me if we had to walk to Billings to go dancing."

He ground his teeth together. She made him feel taller, more masculine, when she looked at him like that. He was struggling with more intense emotions than he'd felt in years. He wanted to grab her and eat her alive. But she needed careful handling. He couldn't be forward with her. Not until he could teach her to trust him. That would take time.

She felt uneasy when he scowled like that. "Sorry," she said. "I didn't mean to blurt that out and upset you . . ."

"You make me feel good, Jake," he interrupted. "I'm not upset. Well, not for the reasons you're thinking, anyway."

"What reasons upset you?"

He sighed. "To be blunt, I'd like to back you into the truck and kiss you half to death." He smiled wryly at her shocked expression. "Won't do it," he promised. "Just telling you what I really feel.

Honesty is a sideline with most people. It's first on my list of necessities."

"Mine, too. It's okay. I like it when you're up-front."

"You're the same way," he pointed out.

"I guess so. Maybe I'm too blunt, sometimes."

He smiled. "I'd call it being forthright. I like it."

She beamed. "Thanks."

He checked his watch. "Got to go." He opened the door for her and waited until she jumped up into the cab and fastened her seat belt before he closed it.

"It impresses me that I didn't have to tell you to put that on," he said as he started the engine, nodding toward her seat belt. "I don't ride with people who refuse to wear them. I work wrecks. Some of them are horrific, and the worst fatalities are when people don't have on seat belts."

"I've heard that."

He pulled out onto the highway. "Here we go, Jake. Our first date." He grinned. "Our uncles are probably laughing their ghostly heads off."

"I wouldn't doubt it." She sighed. "Still, it wasn't nice of either of them to rig the wills like that."

"I guess they didn't expect to die for years and years," he commented. "Maybe it was a joke. They expected the lawyer to tell us long before they died. Except he died first and his partner had no sense of humor."

"I don't know. Our uncles did like to manipulate people."

"Too much," he murmured. "They browbeat poor old Dan Harper into marrying Daisy Kane, and he was miserable. They thought she was a sweet, kind girl who'd never want anything more than to go on living in Hollister for the rest of her life."

"Then she discovered a fascination for microscopes, got a science degree and moved to New York City to work in a research lab. Dan wouldn't leave Hollister, so they got a divorce. Good thing they didn't have kids, I guess."

"I guess. Especially with Dan living in a whiskey bottle these days."

She glanced at him. "Maybe some women mature late."

He glanced back. "You going to develop a fascination with microscopes and move to New York?" he asked suspiciously.

She laughed out loud. "I hope not. I hate cities."

He grinned again. "Me, too. Just checking."

"Besides, how could I leave Sammy? I'm sure there isn't an apartment in a big city that would let you keep a calf in it."

He laughed. "Well, they would. But only in the fridge. Or the freezer."

"You bite your tongue!" she exclaimed. "Nobody's eating my cow!"

He frowned thoughtfully. "Good point. I'm not

exactly sure I know how to field dress a cow. A steer, sure. But cows are, well, different."

She glared at him. "You are not field dressing Sammy, so forget it."

He sighed. "There go my dreams of a nice steak."

"You can get one at the restaurant in town anytime you like. Sammy is for petting, not eating."

"If you say so."

"I do!"

He loved to wind her up and watch the explosion. She was so full of life, so enthusiastic about everything new. He enjoyed being with her. There were all sorts of places he could take her. He was thinking ahead. Far ahead.

"You're smirking," she accused. "What are you thinking about?"

"I was just remembering how excited you get about new things," he confessed. "I was thinking of places we could go together."

"You were?" she asked, surprised. And flattered.

He smiled at her. "I've never dated anybody regularly," he said. "I mean, I've had dates. But this is different." He searched for a way to put into words what he was thinking.

"You mean, because we're sort of being forced into it by the wills."

He frowned. "No. That's not what I mean." He stopped at an intersection and glanced her way. "I haven't had regular dates with a woman I've known well for years and years," he said after a minute. "Somebody I like."

She beamed. "Oh."

He chuckled as he pulled out onto the long highway that led to Billings. "We've had our verbal cut-and-thrust encounters, but despite that sharp tongue, I enjoy being with you."

She laughed. "It's not that sharp."

"Not to me. I understand there's a former customer of the florist shop where you worked who could write a testimonial for you about your use of words in a free-for-all."

She flushed and fiddled with her purse. "He was obnoxious."

"Actually they said he was just trying to ask you out."

"It was the way he went about it," she said curtly. "I don't think I've ever had a man talk to me like that in my whole life."

"I don't think he'll ever use the same language to any other woman, if it's a consolation." He teased. "So much for his inflated ego."

"He thought he was irresistible," she muttered. "Bragging about his fast new car and his dad's bank balance, and how he could get any woman he wanted." Her lips set. "Well, he couldn't get this one."

"Teenage boys have insecurities," he said. "I can speak with confidence on that issue, because I used to be one myself." He glanced at her with twinkling black eyes. "They're puff adders."

She blinked. "Excuse me?"

"I've never seen one myself, but I had a buddy in the service who was from Georgia. He told me about them. They're these snakes with insecurities."

She burst out laughing. "Snakes with insecurities?"

He nodded. "They're terrified of people. So if humans come too close to them, they rise up on their tails and weave back and forth and blow out their throats and start hissing. You know, imitating a cobra. Most of the time, people take them at face value and run away."

"What if people stand their ground and don't run?"

He laughed. "They faint."

"They faint?"

He nodded. "Dead away, my buddy said. He took a friend home with him. They were walking through the fields when a puff adder rose up and did his act for the friend. The guy was about to run for it when my buddy walked right up to the snake and it fainted dead away. I hear his family is still telling the story with accompanying sound effects and hilarity."

"A fainting snake." She sighed. "What I've missed, by spending my whole life in Montana. I wouldn't have known any better, either, though. I've never seen a cobra."

"They have them in zoos," he pointed out.

"I've never been to a zoo."

"What?"

"Well, Billings is a long way from Hollister and I've never had a vehicle I felt comfortable about getting there in." She grimaced. "This is a very deserted road, most of the time. If I broke down, I'd worry about who might stop to help me."

He gave her a covert appraisal. She was such a private person. She kept things to herself. Remembering her uncle and his weak heart, he wasn't surprised that she'd learned to do that.

"You couldn't talk to your uncle about most things, could you, Jake?" he wondered out loud.

"Not really," she agreed. "I was afraid of upsetting him, especially after his first heart attack."

"So you learned to keep things to yourself."

"I pretty much had to. I've never had close girlfriends, either."

"Most of the girls your age are married and have kids, except the ones who went into the military or moved to cities."

She nodded. "I'm a throwback to another era, when women lived at home until they married. Gosh, the world has changed," she commented.

"It sure has," he agreed. "When I was a boy, television sets were big and bulky and in cabinets. Now they're so thin and light that people can hang them on walls. And my iPod does everything a television can do, right down to playing movies and giving me news and weather."

She frowned. "That wasn't what I meant, exactly."

He raised his eyebrows.

"I mean, that women seem to want careers and men in volume."

He cleared his throat.

"That didn't come out right." She laughed self-consciously. "It just seems to me that women are more like the way men used to be. They don't want commitment. They have careers and they live with men. I heard a newscaster say that marriage is too retro a concept for modern people."

"There have always been people who lived out of the mainstream, Jake," he said easily. "It's a choice."

"It wouldn't be mine," she said curtly. "I think people should get married and stay married and raise children together."

"Now that's a point of view I like."

She studied him curiously. "Do you want kids?"

He smiled. "Of course. Don't you?"

She averted her eyes. "Well, yes. Someday."

He sighed. "I keep forgetting how young you are. You haven't really had time to live yet."

"You mean, get fascinated with microscopes and move to New York City," she said with a grin.

He laughed. "Something like that, maybe."

"I could never see stuff in microscopes in high

school," she recalled. "I was so excited when I finally found what I thought was an organism and the teacher said it was an air bubble. That's all I ever managed to find." She grimaced. "I came within two grade points of failing biology. As it was, I had the lowest passing grade in my whole class."

"But you can cook like an angel," he pointed out.

She frowned. "What does that have to do with microscopes?"

"I'm making an observation," he replied. "We all have skills. Yours is cooking. Somebody else's might be science. It would be a pretty boring world if we all were good at the same things."

"I see."

He smiled. "You can crochet, too. My grandmother loved her crafts, like you do. She could make quilts and knit sweaters and crochet afghans. A woman of many talents."

"They don't seem to count for much in the modern world," she replied.

"Have you ever really looked at the magazine rack, Jake?" he asked, surprised. "There are more magazines on handicrafts than there are on rock stars, and that's saying something."

"I hadn't noticed." She looked around. They were just coming into Billings. Ahead, she could see the awesome outline of the Rimrocks, where the airport was located, in the distance. "We're here?" she exclaimed.

"It's not so far from home," he said lazily.

"Not at the speed you go, no," she said impudently.

He laughed. "There wasn't any traffic and we aren't overly blessed with highway patrols at this hour of the night."

"You catch speeders, and you're local law enforcement," she pointed out.

"I don't catch them on the interstate unless they're driving on it through my town," he replied. "And it's not so much the speed that gets them caught, either. It's the way they're driving. You can be safe at high speeds and dangerous at low ones. Weaving in and out of traffic, riding people's bumpers, running stop signs, that sort of thing."

"I saw this television program where an experienced traffic officer said that what scared him most was to see a driver with both hands white-knuckled and close together on the steering wheel."

He nodded. "There are exceptions, but it usually means someone who's insecure and afraid of the vehicle."

"You aren't."

He shrugged. "I've been driving since I was twelve. Kids grow up early when they live on ranches. Have to learn how to operate machinery, like tractors and harvesters."

"Our ranch doesn't have a harvester."

"That's because our ranch can't afford one," he

said, smiling. "But we can always borrow one from neighbors."

"Small towns are such nice places," she said dreamily. "I love it that people will loan you a piece of equipment that expensive just because they like you."

"I imagine there are people in cities who would do the same, Jake, but there's not much use for them there."

She laughed. "No, I guess not."

He turned the corner and pulled into a parking lot next to a long, low building. There was a neon sign that said Red's Tavern.

"It's a bar?" she asked.

"It's a dance club. They do serve alcohol, but not on the dance floor."

"Theodore, I don't think I've ever been in a bar in my life."

"Not to worry, they won't force you to drink anything alcoholic," he told her, tongue-in-cheek. "And if they tried, I'd have to call local law and have them arrested. You're underage."

"Local law?"

"I'm not sanctioned to arrest people outside my own jurisdiction," he reminded her. "But you could make a citizen's arrest. Anybody can if they see a crime being committed. It's just that we don't advise it. Could get you killed, depending on the circumstances."

"I see what you mean."

He got out and opened her door, lifting her gently down from the truck by the waist. He held her just in front of him for a minute, smiling into her soft eyes. "You're as light as a feather," he commented softly. "And you smell pretty."

A shocked little laugh left her throat. "I smell pretty?"

"Yes. I remember my grandmother by her scent. She wore a light, flowery cologne. I recognize it if I smell it anywhere. She always smelled so good."

Her hands rested lightly on his broad shoulders. He was very strong. She loved his strength, his size. She smiled into his dark eyes. "You smell good, too. Spicy."

He nuzzled her nose with his. "Thanks."

She sighed and slid her arms around his neck. She tucked her face into his throat. "I feel so safe with you," she said softly. "Like nothing could ever hurt me."

"Now, Jake, that's not the sort of thing a man likes to hear."

She lifted her head, surprised. "Why?"

He pursed his lips. "We want to hear that we're dangerous and exciting, that we stir you up and make you nervous."

"You do?"

"It's a figure of speech."

She searched his eyes. "You don't want me to feel comfortable with you?" she faltered.

"You don't understand what I'm talking about, do you?" he wondered gently.

"No . . . not really. I'm sorry."

It was early days yet, he reminded himself. It was disappointing that she wasn't shaky when he touched her. But, then, she kept secrets. There must be a reason why she was so icy inside herself.

He set her down but he didn't let her go. "Some things have to be learned," he said.

"Learned."

He framed her face with his big, warm hands. "Passion, for instance."

She blinked.

It was like describing ice to a desert nomad. He smiled wistfully. "You haven't ever been kissed in such a way that you'd die to have it happen again?"

She shook her head. Her eyes were wide and innocent, unknowing. She flushed a little and shifted restlessly.

"But you have been kissed in such a way that you'd rather undergo torture than have it happen again," he said suddenly.

She caught her breath. He couldn't know! He couldn't!

His black eyes narrowed on her face. "Something happened to you, Jake. Something bad. It made you lock yourself away from the world. And it wasn't your experience with the traveling auditor."

"You can't know . . . !"

"Of course not," he interrupted impatiently. "You know I don't pry. But I've been in law enforcement a long time, and I've learned to read people pretty good. You're afraid of me when I get too close to you."

She bit down hard on her lower lip. She drew blood.

"Stop that," he said in a tender tone, touching her lower lip where her teeth had savaged it. "I'm not going to try to browbeat you into telling me something you don't want to. But I wish you trusted me enough to talk to me about it. You know I'm not judgmental."

"It doesn't have anything to do with that."

He cocked his head. "Can't you tell me?"

She hesitated noticeably. She wanted to. She really wanted to. But . . .

He bent and kissed her eyelids shut. "Don't. We have all the time in the world. When you're ready to talk, I'll listen."

She drew in a long, labored breath and laid her forehead against his suit coat. "You're the nicest man I've ever known."

He smiled over her head. "Well, that's a start, I guess."

She smiled, too. "It's a start."

Chapter 4

It was the liveliest place Jillian had ever been to. The dance band was on a platform at the end of a long, wide hall with a polished wooden floor. Around the floor were booths, not tables, and there was a bar in the next room with three bartenders, two of whom were female.

The music was incredible. It was Latin with a capital *L,* pulsing and narcotic. On the dance floor, people were moving to the rhythm. Some had on jeans and boots, others were wearing ensembles that would have done justice to a club in New York City. Still others, apparently too intimidated by the talent being displayed on the dance floor, were standing on the perimeter of the room, clapping and smiling.

"Wow," Jillian said, watching a particularly talented couple, a silver-haired lean and muscular man with a willowy blonde woman somewhat younger than he was. They whirled and pivoted, laughing, with such easy grace and elegance that she couldn't take her eyes off them.

"That's Red Jernigan," he told her, indicating the silver-haired man, whose thick, long hair was in a ponytail down his back.

"He isn't redheaded," she pointed out.

He gave her an amused look. "It doesn't refer to his coloring," he told her. "They called him that because in any battle, he was the one most likely to come out bloody."

She gasped. "Oh."

"I have some odd friends." He shrugged, then smiled. "You'll get used to them."

He was saying something profound about their future. She was confused, but she returned his smile anyway.

The dance ended and Theodore tugged her along with him to the dance floor, where the silver-haired man and the blonde woman were catching their breath.

"Hey, Red," he greeted the other man, who grinned and gripped his hand. "Good to see you."

"About time you came up for a visit." Red's dark eyes slid to the small blonde woman beside the police chief. His eyebrows arched.

"This is Jillian," Theodore said gently. "And this is Red Jernigan."

"I'm Melody," the pretty blonde woman said, introducing herself. "Nice to meet you."

Red slid his arm around the woman and pulled her close. "Nice to see Ted going around with somebody," he observed. "It's painful to see a man come alone to a dance club and refuse to dance with anyone except the owner's wife."

"Well, I don't like most modern women." Theodore excused himself. He smiled down at a grinning Jillian. "I like Jake, here."

"Jake?" Red asked, blinking.

"He's always called me that," Jillian sighed. "I've known him a long time."

"She has," Theodore drawled, smiling. "She likes cattle."

"I don't," Melody laughed. "Smelly things."

"Oh, but they're not smelly if they're kept clean," Jillian protested at once. "Sammy is always neat."

"Her calf," Theodore explained.

"Is he a bull?" Red asked.

"She's a heifer," Jillian inserted. "A little black baldy."

Red and Melody were giving her odd looks.

"As an acquaintance of mine in Jacobsville, Texas, would say," Red told them, "if Johnny Cash could sing about a boy named Sue, a person can have a girl animal with a boy's name." He leaned closer. "He has a female border collie named Bob."

They burst out laughing.

"Well, don't stand over here with us old folks," Red told them. "Get out there with the younger generation and show them how to tango."

"You aren't old, Bud," Theodore told his friend with twinkling eyes. "You're just a hair slower than you used to be, but with the same skills."

"Which I hope I'm never called to use again," Red replied solemnly. "I'm still on reserve status."

"I know."

"Red was a bird colonel in spec ops," Theodore explained to Jillian later when they were sitting at a table sampling the club's exquisitely cooked seasoned steak and fancy baked sweet potatoes, which it was as famous for as its dance band.

"And he still is?" she asked.

He nodded. "He can do more with recruits than any man I ever knew, and without browbeating them. He just encourages. Of course, there are times when he has to get a little more creative, with the wilder sort."

"Creative?"

He grinned. "There was this giant of a kid from Milwaukee who was assigned to his unit in the field. Kid played video games and thought he knew more about strategy and tactics than Red did. So Red turns him loose on the enemy, but with covert backup."

"What happened?" she asked, all eyes.

"The kid walked right into an enemy squad and froze in his tracks. It's one thing to do that on a computer screen. Quite another to confront armed men in real life. They were aiming their weapons at him when Red led a squad in to recover him. Took about two minutes for them to eliminate the threat and get Commando Carl back to his own lines." He shook his head. "In the excitement, the kid had, shall we say, needed access to a restroom and didn't have one. So they hung a nickname on him that stuck."

"Tell me!"

He chuckled. "Let's just say that it suited him.

He took it in his stride, sucked up his pride, learned to follow orders and became a real credit to the unit. He later became mayor of a small town somewhere up north, where he's still known, to a favored few, as 'Stinky.'"

She laughed out loud.

"Actually, he was in good company. I read in a book on World War II that one of our better known generals did the same thing when his convoy ran into a German attack. Poor guy. I'll bet Stinky cringed every time he saw that other general's book on a rack."

"I don't doubt it."

She sipped her iced tea and smiled. "This is really good food," she said. "I've never had a steak that was so tender, not even from beef my uncle raised."

"This is Kobe beef," he pointed out. "Red gets it from Japan. God knows how," he added.

"I read about those. Don't they actually massage the beef cattle?"

"Pamper them," he agreed. "You should try that sweet potato," he advised. "It's really a unique combination of spices they use."

She frowned, picking at it with her fork. "I've only ever had a couple of sweet potatoes, and they were mostly tasteless."

"Just try it."

She put the fork into it, lifted it dubiously to her lips and suddenly caught her breath when the taste hit her tongue like dynamite. “Wow!” she exclaimed. “What do they call this?”

“Red calls it ‘the ultimate jalapeño-brown-sugar-sweet-potato delight.’ ”

“It’s heavenly!”

He chuckled. “It is, isn’t it? The jalapeño gives it a kick like a mule, but it’s not so hot that even tenderfeet wouldn’t eat it.”

“I would never have thought of such a combination. And I thought I was a good cook.”

“You are a good cook, Jake,” he said. “The best I ever knew.”

She blushed. “Thanks, Theodore.”

He cocked his head. “I guess it would kill you to shorten that.”

“Shorten what?”

“My name. Most people call me Ted.”

She hesitated with the fork in midair. She searched his black eyes for a long time. “Ted,” she said softly.

His jaw tautened. He hadn’t expected it to have that effect on him. She had a soft, sweet, sexy voice when she let herself relax with him. She made his name sound different; special. New.

“I like the way you say it,” he said, when she gave him a worried look. “It’s—” he searched for a word that wouldn’t intimidate her “—it’s stimulating.”

“Stimulating.” She didn’t understand.

He put down his fork with a long sigh. "Something happened to you," he said quietly. "You don't know me well enough to talk to me about it. Or maybe you're afraid that I might go after the man who did it."

She was astounded. She couldn't even manage words. She just stared at him, shocked.

"I'm in law enforcement," he reminded her. "After a few years, you read body language in a different way than most people do. Abused children have a look, a way of dressing and acting, one that's obvious to a cop."

She went white. She bit her lower lip and her fingers toyed with her fork as she stared at it, fighting tears.

His big hand curled around hers, gently. "I wish you could tell me. I think it would help you."

She looked up into quiet, patient eyes. "You wouldn't . . . think badly of me?"

"For God's sake," he groaned. "Are you nuts?"

She blinked.

He grimaced. "Sorry. I didn't mean to put it that way. Nothing I found out about you would change the way I feel. If that's why you're reluctant."

"You're sure?"

He glared at her.

She lowered her eyes and curled her small hand into his big one, a trusting gesture that touched him in a new and different way.

"When I was fifteen, Uncle John had this

young man he got to do odd jobs around here. He was a drifter, very intelligent. He seemed like a nice, trustworthy person to have around the house. Then one day Uncle John felt bad and went to bed, left me with the hired man in the kitchen."

Her jaw clenched. "At first, he was real helpful. Wanted to put out the trash for me and sweep the floor. I thought it was so nice of him. Then all of a sudden, he asked what was my bra size and if I wore nylon panties."

Theodore's eyes began to flash.

She swallowed. "I was so shocked I didn't know what to do or say. I thought it was some sick joke. Until he tried to take my clothes off, mumbling all the time that I needed somebody to teach me about men and he was the perfect person, because he'd had so many virgins."

"Good God!"

"Uncle John was asleep. There was nobody to help me. But the Peales lived right down the road, and I knew a back way through the woods to their house. I hit him in a bad place and ran out the door as fast as my legs could carry me. I was almost naked by then." She closed her eyes, shivering with the memory of the terror she'd felt, running and hearing him curse behind her as he crashed through the undergrowth in pursuit.

"I didn't think what danger I might be placing Sassy Peale and her mother and stepsister in, I just knew they'd help me and I was terrified. I banged on the door and Sassy came to it. When she saw how I looked, she ran for the shotgun they kept in the hall closet. By the time the hired man got on the porch, Sassy had the shotgun loaded and aimed at his stomach. She told him if he moved she'd blow him up."

She sipped tea while she calmed a little from the remembered fear. Her hand was shaking, but just a little. Her free hand was still clasped gently in Theodore's.

"He tried to blame it on me, to say I'd flirted and tried to seduce him, but Sassy knew better. She held him at bay until her mother called the police. They took him away." She drew in a breath. "There was a trial. It was horrible, but at least it was in closed session, in the judge's chambers. The hired man plea-bargained. You see, he had priors, many of them. He drew a long jail sentence, but it did at least spare me a public trial." She sipped tea again. "His sister lived over in Wyoming. She came to see me, after the trial." Her eyes closed. "She said I was a slut who had no business putting a sweet, nice guy like him behind bars for years." She managed a smile. "Sassy was in the kitchen when the woman came to the door. She marched into the living room and gave that woman hell. She told her about her innocent brother's priors and how many young girls had suffered because of his inability to control his own desires. She was eloquent. The woman shut up and went away. I never heard from her again." She looked over at him. "Sassy's been my friend ever since. Not a close one, I'm sorry to say. I was so embarrassed at having her know about it that it inhibited me with her and everyone else. Everyone would believe the man's sister, and that I'd asked for it."

His fingers curled closer into hers. "No young woman asks for such abuse," he said softly. "But abusers use that argument to defend themselves. It's a lie, like all their other lies."

"Sometimes," she said, to be fair, "women do lie, and men, innocent men, go to jail for things they didn't do."

"Yes," he agreed. "But more often than not, such lies are found out, and the women themselves are punished for it."

"I guess so."

"I wasn't here when that happened."

"No. You were doing that workshop at the FBI Academy. And I begged the judge not to tell you or anybody else. She was very kind to me."

He looked over her head, his eyes flashing cold and black as he thought what he might have done to the man if he'd been in town. He wasn't interested in Jillian as a woman back then, because she was still almost a child, but he'd always been fond of her. He would have wiped the floor with the man.

His expression made her feel warm inside. “You’d have knocked him up and down main street,” she ventured.

He laughed, surprised, and met her eyes. “Worse than that, probably.” He frowned. “First the hired man, then the accountant.”

“The accountant was my fault,” she confessed. “I never told him how old I was, and I was infatuated with him. He was drinking when he tried to persuade me.” She shook her head. “I can’t believe I even did that.”

He stared at her. “You were a kid, Jake. Kids aren’t known for deep thought.”

She smiled. “Thanks for not being judgmental.”

He shrugged. “I’m such a nice man that I’m never judgmental.”

Her eyebrows arched.

He grinned. “And I really can do the tango. Suppose I teach you?”

She studied his lean, handsome face. “It’s a very, well, sensual sort of dance, they say.”

“Very.” He pursed his lips. “But I’m not an aggressive man. Not in any way that should frighten you.”

She colored a little. “Really?”

“Really.”

She drew in a long breath. “I guess every woman should dance the tango at least once.”

“My thoughts exactly.”

He wiped his mouth on the linen napkin, took a

last sip of the excellent but cooling coffee and got to his feet.

"You have to watch your back on the dance floor, though," he told her as he led her toward it.

"Why is that?"

"When the other women see what a great dancer I am, they'll probably mob you and take me away from you," he teased.

She laughed. "Okay." She leaned toward him. "Are you packing?"

"Are you kidding?" he asked, indicating the automatic nestled at his waist on his belt. "I'm a cop. I'm always packing. And you keep your little hands off my gun," he added sternly. "I don't let women play with it, even if they ask nicely."

"Theodore, I'm scared of guns," she reminded him. "And you know it. That's why *you* come over and sit on the front porch and shoot bottles on stumps, just to irritate me."

"I'll try to reform," he promised.

"Lies."

He put his hand over his heart. "I only lie when I'm salving someone's feelings," he pointed out. "There are times when telling the truth is cruel."

"Oh, yeah? Name one."

He nodded covertly toward a woman against the wall. "Well, if I told that nice lady that her dress looks like she had it painted on at a carnival, she'd probably feel bad."

She bit her lip trying not to laugh. "She probably thinks it looks sexy."

"Oh, no. Sexy is a dress that covers almost everything, but leaves one little tantalizing place bare," he said. "That's why Japanese kimonos have that dip on the back of the neck, that just reveals the nape, when the rest of the woman is covered from head to toe. The Japanese think the nape of the neck is sexy."

"My goodness!" She stared up at him, impressed. "You've been so many places. I've only ever been out of Montana once, when I drove to Oklahoma with Uncle John to a cattle convention. I've never been out of the country at all. You learn a lot about other people when you travel, don't you?"

He nodded. He smiled. "Other countries have different customs. But people are mostly the same everywhere. I've enjoyed the travel most of all, even when I had to do it on business."

"Like the time you flew to London with that detective from Scotland Yard. Imagine a British case that involved a small town like Hollister!" she exclaimed.

"The perpetrator was a murderer who came over here fishing to provide himself with an alibi while his wife committed the crime and blamed it on her absent husband. In the end, they both drew life sentences."

"Who did they kill?" she asked.

"Her cousin who was set to inherit the family estate and about ten million pounds," he said, shaking his head. "The things sensible people will do for money never ceases to amaze me. I mean, it isn't like you can take it with you when you die. And how many houses can you live in? How many cars can you drive?" He frowned. "I think of money the way the Crow and Cheyenne people do. The way most Native Americans do. The man in the tribe who is the most honored is always the poorest, because he gives away everything he has to people who need it more. They're not capitalists. They don't understand societies that equate prestige with money."

"And they share absolutely everything," she agreed. "They don't understand private property."

He laughed. "Neither do I. The woods and the rivers and the mountains are ageless. You can't own them."

"See? That's the Cheyenne in you talking."

He touched her blond hair. "Probably it is. We going to dance, or talk?"

"You're leading, aren't you?"

He tugged her onto the dance floor. "Apparently." He drew her gently to him and then hesitated. After what she'd told him, he didn't want to do anything that would make her uncomfortable. He said so.

"I don't . . . well, I don't feel uncomfortable, like that, with you," she faltered, looking up into his black eyes. She managed a shaky little smile. "I like being close to you." She flushed, afraid she'd been too bold. Or that he'd think she was being forward. Her expression was troubled.

He just smiled. "You can say anything to me," he said gently. "I won't think you're being shallow or vampish. Okay?"

She relaxed. "Okay. Is this going to be hard to learn?"

"Very."

She drew in a long breath. "Then I guess we should get started."

His eyes smiled down at her. "I guess we should."

He walked her around the dance floor, to her amusement, teaching her how the basic steps were done. It wasn't like those exotic tangos she'd seen in movies at first. It was like kindergarten was to education.

She followed his steps, hesitantly at first, then a little more confidently, until she was moving with some elegance.

"Now, this is where we get into the more exotic parts," he said. "It involves little kicks that go between the legs." He leaned to her ear. "I think we should have kids one day, so it's very important that you don't get overenthusiastic with the kicks. And you should also be very careful where you place them."

It took her a minute to understand what he

meant, and then she burst out laughing instead of being embarrassed.

He grinned. "Just playing it safe," he told her. "Ready? This is how you do it."

It was fascinating, the complexity of the movements and the fluid flow of the steps as he paced the dance to the music.

"It doesn't look like this in most movies," she said as she followed his steps.

"That's because it's a stylized version of the tango," he told her. "Most people have no idea how it's supposed to be done. But there are a few movies that go into it in depth. One was made in black and white by a British woman. It's my favorite. Very comprehensive. Even about the danger of the kicks." He chuckled.

"It's Argentinian, isn't it? The dance, I mean."

"You'd have to ask my buddy about that, I'm not sure. I know there are plenty of dance clubs down there that specialize in tango. The thing is, you're supposed to do these dances with strangers. It's as much a social expression as it is a dance."

"Really?"

He nodded. He smiled. "Maybe we should get a bucket and put all our spare change into it. Then, when we're Red's age, we might have enough to buy tickets to Buenos Aires and go dancing."

She giggled. "Oh, I'm sure we'd have the ticket price in twenty or thirty years."

He sighed as he led. "Or forty." He shook his

head. "I've always wanted to travel. I did a good bit of it in the service, but there are plenty of places I'd love to see. Like those ruins in Peru and the pyramids, and the Sonoran desert."

She frowned. "The Sonoran desert isn't exotic."

He smiled. "Sure it is. Do you know, those Saguaro cacti can live for hundreds of years? And that if a limb falls on you, it can kill you because of the weight? You don't think about them being that heavy, but they have a woody spine and limbs to support the weight of the water they store."

"Gosh. How do you know all that?"

He grinned. "The *Science Channel*, the *Discovery Channel*, the *National Geographic Channel* . . ."

She laughed. "I like to watch those, too."

"I don't think I've missed a single nature special," he told her. He gave her a droll look. "Now that should tell you all you need to know about my social life." He grinned.

She laughed, too. "Well, my social life isn't much better. This is the first time I've been on a real date."

His black eyebrows arched.

She flushed. She shrugged. She averted her eyes.

He tilted her face up to his and smiled with a tenderness that made her knees weak. "I heartily approve," he said, "of the fact that you've been saving yourself for me, just like your uncle did," he added outrageously.

She almost bent over double laughing. "No fair."

"Just making the point." He slid his arm around her and pulled her against him. She caught her breath.

He hesitated, his dark eyes searching hers to see if he'd upset her.

"My . . . goodness," she said breathlessly.

He raised his eyebrows.

She averted her eyes and her cheeks took on a glow. She didn't know how to tell him that the sensations she was feeling were unsettling. She could feel the muscles of his chest pressed against her breasts, and it was stimulating, exciting. It was a whole new experience to be held close to a man's body, to feel its warm strength, to smell the elusive, spicy cologne he was wearing.

"You've danced with men before."

"Yes, of course," she confessed. She looked up at him with fascination. "But it didn't, well, it didn't . . . feel like this."

That made him arrogant. His chin lifted and he looked down at her with possession kindling in his eyes.

"Sorry," she said quickly, embarrassed. "I just blurt things out."

He bent his head, so that his mouth was right beside her ear as he eased her into the dance. "It's okay," he said softly.

She bit her lip and laughed nervously.

"Well, it's okay to feel like that with me," he corrected. "But you should know that it's very wrong for you to feel that way with any other man. So you should never dance with anybody but me for the rest of your life."

She burst out laughing again.

He chuckled. "You're a quick study, Jake," he noted as she followed his steps easily. "I think we may become famous locally for this dance once you get used to it."

"You think?" she teased.

He turned her back over his arm, pulled her up, and spun her around with skill. She laughed breathlessly. It was really fun.

"I haven't danced in years," he sighed. "I love to do it, but I'm not much of a party person."

"I'm not, either. I'm much more at home in a kitchen than I am in a club." She grimaced. "That's not very modern, either, for a woman. I always feel that I should be working my way up a corporate ladder somewhere or immersing myself in higher education."

"Would you like to be a corporate leader?"

She made a face. "Not really. Jobs like that are demanding, and you have to want them more than anything. I'm just not ambitious, I guess. Although," she mused, "I think I might like to take a college course."

"What sort?" he asked.

"Anthropology."

He stopped dancing and looked down at her, fascinated. "Why?"

"I like reading about ancient humans, and how archaeologists can learn so much from skeletal material. I go crazy over those *National Geographic* specials on Egypt."

He laughed. "So do I."

"I'd love to see the pyramids. All of them, even those in Mexico and Asia."

"There are pyramids here in the States," he reminded her. "Those huge earthen mounds that primitive people built were the equivalent of pyramids."

She stopped dancing. "Why do you think they built them?"

"I don't know. It's just a guess. But most of the earthen mounds are near rivers. I've always thought maybe they were where the village went to get out of the water when it flooded."

"It's as good a theory as any other," she agreed. "But what about in Egypt? I don't think they had a problem with flooding," she added, tongue in cheek.

"Now, see, there's another theory about that. Thousands of years ago, Egypt was green and almost tropical, with abundant sources of water. So who knows?"

"It was green?" she exclaimed.

He nodded. "There were forests."

"Where did you learn that?"

"I read, too. I think it was in Herodotus. They called him the father of history. He wrote about Egypt. He admitted that the information might not all be factual, but he wrote down exactly what the Egyptian priests told him about their country."

"I'd like to read what he said."

"You can borrow one of my books," he offered. "I have several copies of his *Histories*."

"Why?"

He grimaced. "Because I keep losing them."

She frowned. "How in the world do you lose a book?"

"You'll have to come home with me sometime and see why."

Her eyes sparkled. "Is that an invitation? You know, 'come up and see my books'?"

He chuckled. "No, it's not a pickup line. I really mean it."

"I'd like to."

"You would?" His arm contracted. "When? How about next Saturday? I'll show you my collection of maps, too."

"Maps?" she exclaimed.

He nodded. "I like topo maps, and relief maps, best of all. It helps me to understand where places are located."

She smiled secretively. "We could compare maps."

“What?”

She sighed. “I guess we do have a lot in common. I think I’ve got half the maps Rand McNally ever published!”

Chapter 5

"Well, what do you know?" He laughed. "We're both closet map fanatics."

"And we love ancient history."

"And we love shooting targets from the front porch."

She glowered up at him.

He sighed. "I'll try to reform."

"You might miss and shoot Sammy," she replied.

"I'm a dead shot."

"Anybody can miss once," she pointed out.

"I guess so."

They'd stopped on the dance floor while the band got ready to start the next number. When they did, he whirled her around and they started all over again. Jillian thought she'd never enjoyed anything in her life so much.

Ted walked her to the front door, smiling. "It was a nice first date."

"Yes, it was," she agreed, smiling back. "I've never had so much fun!"

He laughed. She made him feel warm inside. She was such an honest person. She wasn't coy or flirtatious. She just said what she felt. It wasn't a trait he was familiar with.

"What are you thinking?" she asked curiously.

"That I'm not used to people who tell the truth."

She blinked. "Why not?"

"Almost all the people I arrest are innocent," he ticked off. "They were set up by a friend, or it was a case of mistaken identity even when there were eyewitnesses. Oh, and, the police have it in for them and arrest them just to be mean. That's my personal favorite," he added facetiously.

She chuckled. "I guess they wish they were innocent."

"I guess."

She frowned. "There's been some talk about that man you arrested for the bank robbery getting paroled because of a technicality. Is it true?"

His face set in hard lines. "It might be. His attorney said that the judge made an error in his instructions to the jury that prejudiced the case. I've seen men get off in similar situations."

"Ted, he swore he'd kill you if he ever got out," she said worriedly.

He pursed his lips and his dark eyes twinkled. "Frightened for me?"

"Of course I am."

He sighed and pulled her close. "Now, that's exactly the sort of thing that makes a man feel good about himself, when some sweet little woman worries about him."

"I'm not little, I'm not sweet and I don't usually worry," she pointed out.

"It's okay if you worry about me," he teased. "As long as you don't do it excessively."

She toyed with the top button of his unbuttoned jacket. “There are lots of safer professions than being a police chief.”

He frowned. “You’re kidding, right?”

She grimaced. “Ted, Joe Brown’s wife was one of my uncle’s friends. She was married to that deputy sheriff who was shot to death a few years ago. She said that she spent their whole married lives sitting by the phone at night, almost shaking with worry every time he had to go out on a case, hoping and praying that he’d come home alive.”

His hands on her slender waist had tightened unconsciously. “Anyone who marries someone in law enforcement has to live with that possibility,” he said slowly.

She bit her lower lip. She was seeing herself sitting by the phone at night, pacing the floor. She was prone to worry anyway. She was very fond of Ted. She didn’t want him to die. But right now, she wasn’t in love. She had time to think about what she wanted to do with her life. She was sure she should give this a lot of thought before she dived headfirst into a relationship with him that might lead very quickly to marriage. She’d heard people talk about how it was when people became very physical with each other, that it was so addictive that they couldn’t bear to be apart at all. Once that happened, she wouldn’t have a chance to see things rationally.

Ted could almost see the thoughts in her mind. Slowly he released her and stepped back.

She felt the distance, and it was more than physical. He was drawing away in every sense.

She looked up at him. She drew in a long breath. "I'm not sure I'm ready, Ted."

"Ready for what?"

That stiffness in him was disturbing, but she had to be honest. "I'm not sure I'm ready to think about marriage."

His black eyes narrowed. "Jillian, if we don't get married, there's a California developer who's going to make this place into hot real estate with tourist impact, and Sammy could end up on a platter."

She felt those words like a body blow. Her eyes, tormented, met his. "But it's not fair, to rush into something without having time to think about it!" she exclaimed. "The wills didn't say we have to get married tomorrow! There's no real time limit!"

There was, but he wasn't going to push her. She had cold feet. She didn't know him that well, despite the years they'd been acquainted, and she wasn't ready for the physical side of marriage. She had hang-ups, and good reasons to have them.

"Okay," he said after a minute. "Suppose we just get to know each other and let the rest ride for a while?"

"You mean, go on dates and stuff?"

He pursed his lips. "Yes. Dates and stuff."

She noticed how handsome he was. In a crowd, he always stood out. He was a vivid sort of person, not like she was at all. But they did enjoy the same sorts of things and they got along, most of the time.

"I would like to see your place," she said.

"I'll come and get you Saturday morning," he said quietly.

He waited for her answer with bridled impatience. She could see that. He wasn't sure of her at all. She hated being so hesitant, but it was a rushed business. She would have to make a decision in the near future or watch Uncle John's ranch become a resort. It didn't bear thinking about. On the other hand, if she said yes to Ted, it would mean a relationship that she was certain she wasn't ready for.

"Stop gnawing your lip off and say yes," Ted told her. "We'll work out the details as we go along."

She sighed. "Okay, Ted," she said after a minute.

He hadn't realized that he'd been holding his breath. He smiled slowly. She was going to take the chance. It was a start.

"Okay." He frowned. "You don't have any low-cut blouses and jeans that look like you've been poured into them, do you?"

"Ted!"

"Well, I was just wondering," he said. "Because if you do, you can't wear them over at my place. We have a dress code."

"A dress code." She nodded. "So your cowboys have to wear dresses." She nodded again.

He burst out laughing. He bent and kissed her, hard, but impersonally, and walked down the steps. "I'll see you Saturday."

"You call that a kiss?" she yelled after him, and shocked herself with the impertinent remark that had jumped out of her so impulsively.

But he didn't react to it the way she expected. He just threw up his hand and kept walking.

They worked side by side in his kitchen making lunch. He was preparing an omelet while she made cinnamon toast and fried bacon.

"Breakfast for lunch," she scoffed.

"Hey, I very often have breakfast for supper, if I've been out on a case," he said indignantly. "There's no rule that says you have to have breakfast in the morning."

"I suppose not."

"See, you don't know how to break rules."

She gasped. "You're a police chief! You shouldn't be encouraging anybody to break rules."

"It's okay as long as it's only related to food," he replied.

She laughed, shaking her head.

"You going to turn that bacon anytime soon?" he asked, nodding toward it, "or do you really like it raw on one side and black on the other?"

"If you don't like it that way, you could fry it yourself."

"I do omelets," he pointed out. "I don't even eat bacon."

"What?"

"Pig meat," he muttered.

"I like bacon!"

"Good. Then you can eat it. I've got a nice country ham all carved up and cooked in the fridge. I'll have that with mine."

"Ham is pig meat, too!"

"I think of it as steak with a curly tail," he replied.

She burst out laughing. He was so different off the job. She'd seen him walking down the sidewalk in town, somber and dignified, almost unapproachable. Here, at home, he was a changed person.

"What are you brooding about?" he wondered.

"Was I? I was just thinking how different you are at home than at work."

"I should hope so," he sighed, as he took the omelet up onto a platter. "I mean, think of the damage to my image if I cooked omelets for the prisoners."

"Chief Barnes used to," she said. "I remember Uncle John talking about what a sweet man he was. He'd take the prisoners himself to funerals when they had family members die, and in those days, when the jail was down the hall from the police department, he'd cook for them, too."

"He was a kind man," Ted agreed solemnly.

"To think that it was one of the prisoners who killed him," she added quietly as she turned the bacon. "Of all the ironies."

"The man was drunk at the time," Ted said. "And, if you recall, he killed himself just a few weeks later while he was waiting for trial. He left a note saying he didn't want to put the chief's family through any more pain."

"Everybody thought that was so odd," she said. "But people forget that murderers are just like everybody else. They aren't born planning to kill people."

"That's true. Sometimes it's alcohol or drugs that make them do it. Other times it's an impulse they can't control. Although," he added, "there are people born without a conscience. They don't mind killing. I've seen them in the military. Not too many, thank goodness, but they come along occasionally."

"Your friend who was a sniper, was he like that?"

"Not at all," he said. "He was trained to think of it as just a skill. It was only later, when it started to kill his soul, that he realized what was happening to him. That was when he got out."

"How in the world did he get into law enforcement, with such a background?" she wondered.

He chuckled. "Uncle Sam often doesn't know when his left hand is doing something different than his right one," he commented. "Government agencies have closed files."

"Oh. I get it. But those files aren't closed to everyone, are they?"

"They're only accessible to people with top-secret military clearance." He glanced at her amusedly. "Never knew a civilian, outside the executive branch, who even had one."

"That makes sense."

He pulled out her chair for her.

"Thank you," she said, with surprise in her tone.

"I'm impressing you with my good manners," he pointed out as he sat down across from her and put a napkin in his lap.

"I'm very impressed." She tasted the omelet, closed her eyes and sighed. "And not only with your manners. Ted, this is delicious!"

He grinned. "Thanks."

"What did you put in it?" she asked, trying to decide what combination of spices he'd used to produce such a taste.

"Trade secret."

"You can tell me," she coaxed. "After all, we're almost engaged."

"The 'almost' is why I'm not telling," he retorted. "If things don't work out, you'll be using my secret spices in your own omelets for some other man."

"I could promise."

"You could, but I'm not telling."

She sighed. “Well, it’s delicious, anyway.”

He chuckled. “The bacon’s not bad, either,” he conceded, having forgone the country ham that would need warming. He was hungry.

“Thanks.” She lifted a piece of toast and gave it a cold look. “Shame we can’t say the same for the toast. Sorry. I was busy trying not to burn the bacon, so I burned the toast instead.”

“I don’t eat toast.”

“I do, but I don’t think I will this time.” She pushed the toast aside.

After they ate, he walked her around the property. He only had a few beef steers in the pasture. He’d bought quite a few Angus cattle with his own uncle, and they were at the ranch that Jillian had shared with her uncle John. She was pensive as she strolled beside him, absently stripping a dead branch of leaves, thinking about the fate of Uncle John’s prize beef if she didn’t marry Ted sometime soon.

“Deep thoughts?” he asked, hands in the pockets of his jeans under his shepherd’s coat.

She frowned. She was wearing her buckskin jacket. One of the pieces of fringe caught on a limb and she had to stop to disentangle it. “I was thinking about that resort,” she confessed.

“Here. Let me.” He stopped and removed the branch from the fringe. “Do you know why these jackets always had fringe?”

She looked up at him, aware of his height and

strength so close to her. He smelled of tobacco and coffee and fir trees. "Not really."

He smiled. "When the old-timers needed something to tie up a sack with, they just pulled off a piece of fringe and used that. Also, the fringe collects water and drips it away from the body."

"My goodness!"

"My grandmother was full of stories like that. Her grandfather was a fur trapper. He lived in the Canadian wilderness. He was French. He married a Blackfoot woman."

She smiled, surprised. "But you always talk about your Cheyenne heritage."

"That's because my other grandmother was Cheyenne. I have interesting bloodlines."

Her eyes sketched his high-cheekboned face, his black eyes and hair and olive complexion. "They combined to make a very handsome man."

"Me?" he asked, surprised.

She grinned. "And not a conceited bone in your body, either, Ted."

He smiled down at her. "Not much to be conceited about."

"Modest, too."

He shrugged. He touched her cheek with his fingertips. "You have beautiful skin."

Her eyebrows arched. "Thank you."

"You get that from your mother," he said gently. "I remember her very well. I was only a boy when she died, but she was well-known locally. She was the best cook in two counties. She was always the first to sit with anyone sick, or to take food when there was a funeral."

"I only know about her through my uncle," she replied. "My uncle loved her. She was his only sister, much older than he was. She and my father had me unexpectedly, late in life."

Which, he thought, had been something of a tragedy.

"And then they both died of the flu, when I was barely crawling," she sighed. "I never knew either of them." She looked up. "You did at least know your parents, didn't you?"

He nodded. "My mother died of a stroke in her early thirties," he said. "My father was overseas, working for an oil corporation as a roughneck, when there was a bombing at the installation and he died. My grandmother took me in, and my uncle moved in to help support us."

"Neither of us had much of a childhood," she said. "Not that our relatives didn't do all they could for us," she added quickly. "They loved us. Lots of orphaned kids have it a lot worse."

"Yes, they do," he agreed solemnly. "That's why we have organizations that provide for orphaned kids."

"If I ever get rich," she commented, "I'm going to donate to those."

He grinned. "I already do. To a couple, at least."

She leaned back against a tree and closed her

eyes, drinking in the sights and sounds and smells of the woods. "I love winter. I know it isn't a popular season," she added. "It's cold and there's a lot of snow. But I enjoy it. I can smell the smoke from fireplaces and woodstoves. If I close my eyes, it reminds me of campfires. Uncle John used to take me camping with him when I was little, to hunt deer."

"Which you never shot."

She opened her eyes and made a face. "I'm not shooting Bambi."

"Bull."

"People shouldn't shoot animals."

"That attitude back in colonial times would have seen you starve to death," he pointed out. "It's not like those old-timers could go to a grocery store and buy meat and vegetables. They had to hunt and garden or die."

She frowned. "I didn't think about that."

"In fact," he added, "people who refused to work were turned out of the forts into the wilderness. Some stole food from the Indians and were killed for it. Others starved or froze to death. It was a hard life."

"Why did they do it?" she wondered aloud. "Why leave their families and their homes and get on rickety old ships and go to a country they'd never even seen?"

"A lot of them did it to escape debtor's prison," he said. "They had debts they couldn't pay. A few years over here working as an indentured servant and they could be free and have money to buy their own land. Or the people they worked for might give them an acre or two, if they were generous."

"What about when the weather took their crops and they had nothing to eat?"

"There are strings of graves over the eastern seaboard of pilgrims who starved," he replied. "A sad end to a hopeful beginning. This is a hostile land when it's stripped of supermarkets and shopping centers."

A silence fell between them, during which he stared at the small rapids in the stream nearby. "That freezes over in winter," he said. "It looks pretty."

"I'd like to see it then."

He turned. "I'll bring you over here."

She smiled. "Okay."

His black eyes looked long and deep into hers across the distance, until she felt as if something snapped inside her. She caught her breath and forced her eyes away.

Ted didn't say anything. He just smiled. And started walking again.

She loved it that he didn't pressure her into a more physical relationship. It gave her a breathing space that she desperately needed.

He took her to a play in Billings the following weekend, a modern parody of an old play about two murderous old women and their assorted crazy relatives.

She laughed until her sides ached. Later, as they were driving home, she realized that it had been a long time since she'd been so amused by anything.

"I'm so glad I never had relatives like that," she ventured.

He laughed. "Me, too. The murderous cousin with the spooky face was a real pain, wasn't he?"

"His associate was even crazier."

She sat back against the seat, her eyes closed, still smiling. "It was a great play. Thanks for asking me."

"I was at a loose end," he commented. "We have busy weekends and slow weekends. This was a very slow one, nothing my officers couldn't handle on their own."

That was a reminder, and not a very pleasant one, of what he did for a living. She frowned in the darkness of the cab, broken only by the blue light of the instrument panel. "Ted, haven't you ever thought about doing something else for a living?"

"Like what?" he asked. "Teaching chemistry to high school students?"

He made a joke of it, but she didn't laugh. "You're not likely to be killed doing that."

"I guess you don't keep up with current events," he remarked solemnly, and proceeded to remind her of several terrible school shootings.

She grimaced. "Yes, but those are rare incidents. You make enemies in your work. What if somebody you locked up gets out and tries to kill you?"

"It goes with the job," he said laconically. "So far, I've been lucky."

Lucky. But it might not last forever. Could she see herself sitting by the phone every night of her life, waiting for that horrible call?

"You're dwelling on anticipation of the worst," he said, glancing her way. "How in the world do you think people get by who have loved ones with chronic illness or life-threatening conditions?"

She looked at him in the darkness. "I've never thought about it."

"My grandmother had cancer," he reminded her. "Had it for years. If I'd spent that time sitting in a chair, brooding on it, what sort of life would it have been for her?"

She frowned. "Lonely."

"Exactly. I knew it could happen, anytime. But I lived from day to day, just like she did. After a while, I got used to the idea, like she did, and we went on with our lives. It was always there, in the background, but it was something we just—" he searched for the word "—lived with. That's how husbands and wives of people in law enforcement and the military deal with it."

It was a new concept for her, living with a terrifying reality and getting used to it.

"You're very young," he said heavily. "It would be harder for you."

It probably would. She didn't answer him. It was something new to think about.

He walked her up the steps to her front door. He looked good in a suit, she thought, smiling.

"What are you thinking?" he teased.

"That you look very elegant in a suit."

He shrugged. "It's a nice suit."

"It's a nice man wearing it."

"Thanks. I like your dress."

She grinned. "It's old, but I like the color. It's called Rose Dust."

He fingered the lacy collar. He wouldn't have told her, because it would hurt her feelings, but it looked like the sort of dress a high school girl would wear. It wasn't sophisticated, or even old enough for her now. But he just smiled.

"Nice color," he agreed.

She cocked her head, feeling reckless. "Going to kiss me?" she asked.

"I was thinking about it."

"And what did you decide?"

He stuck his hands in his pockets and just smiled down at her. "That would be rushing things a little too much," he said gently. "You want to date and get to know each other. I think that's a good idea. Plenty of time for the other, later."

"Well, my goodness!"

"Shocked by my patience, are you?" he asked with a grin. "Me, too."

"Very."

His eyes were old and wise. "When things get physical, there's a difference in the way two people are, together. There's no time to step back and look at how things really are."

She nodded. "You mean, like Sassy and her husband, John Callister, when they first got married. They couldn't stand to be apart, even for an hour or two. They still pretty much go everywhere together. And they're always standing close, or touching."

"That's what I mean."

She frowned. "I haven't ever felt like that," she said.

He smiled. "I noticed."

She flushed. "I'm sorry, I just blurt things out . . ."

"I don't mind that you're honest," he said. "It helps. A lot."

She bit her lower lip. "I'd give anything if Uncle John hadn't hired that man to come work for him."

"I'm sure your uncle felt the same way. I'm surprised that he never told me about it," he added curtly.

"I imagine he thought you'd hold him responsible for it. He blamed himself," she added softly. "He never stopped apologizing." She sighed. "It didn't help very much."

"Of course it didn't." He stepped closer and tilted her chin up. "You'll deal with it. If you don't think you can, there are some good psychologists. Our department works with two, who live in Billings."

She made a face. "I don't think I could talk about something like that to a total stranger."

He stared at her for a long time. "How about me?" he asked suddenly. "Could you talk about it to me?"

Chapter 6

Jillian stared up at him with conflicting emotions. But after a minute she nodded. “I think I could,” she replied finally.

He beamed. His black eyes were twinkling. “That’s a major step forward.”

“Think so?”

“I know so.”

She moved a step closer. “I enjoyed tonight. Thank you.”

He gave her a teasing look and moved a step away. “I did, too, and I’ll thank you to keep your distance. I don’t want to be an object of lust to a single woman who lives alone.”

She gasped theatrically. “You do so!”

“I do?”

“Absolutely!” she agreed. She grinned. “But not right now. Right?”

He laughed. “Not right now.” He bent and brushed a lazy kiss against her forehead. “Get some sleep. I’ll call you Monday.”

“You do that. Not early,” she added, without telling him why. She had a secret, and she wasn’t sharing it.

“Not early,” he agreed. “Good night.”

“Good night, Ted.”

He bounded down the steps, jumped in his truck and sat there deliberately until she got the message. She went inside, locked the door and turned off the porch light. Only then did he drive away. It made her feel safe, that attitude of his. Probably it was instinctive, since he was in law enforcement, but she liked it. She liked it very much.

Snow came the next morning. Jillian loved it. She drove slowly, so that she didn't slip off the road. But there wasn't much traffic, and she lived close to town. It was easier than she expected to get in on the country roads.

When she left again, at noon, it was a different story. The snow had come fast and furiously, and she could barely crawl along the white highway. The road crews had been busy, spreading sand and gravel, but there were icy spots just the same.

She hesitated to go all the way back to the ranch when she couldn't see the road ahead for the blinding snow, so she pulled into the town's only restaurant and cut off the engine.

"Well," she said to herself, "I guess if worse comes to worst, they might let me sleep in a booth in the restaurant." She laughed at the imagery.

She grabbed her purse and got out, grateful for her high-heeled cowboy boots that made it easier to get a foothold in the thick, wet snow. This was the kind that made good snowmen. She thought she might make one when she finally got home. A calf, perhaps, to look like Sammy. She laughed. Ted would howl at that, if she did it.

She opened the door of the restaurant and walked right into a nightmare. Davy Harris, the man who had almost raped her, was standing by the counter, paying his bill. He was still thin and nervous-looking, with straggly brown hair and pale eyes. He looked at her with mingled distaste and hatred.

"Well, well, I hoped I might run into you again," he said in a voice dripping with venom. "I don't guess you expected to see me, did you, Jillian? Not the man you put in prison for trying to kiss you!"

The owner of the restaurant knew Jillian, and liked her, but he was suddenly giving her a very odd look. There was another customer behind him, one who'd known Jillian's uncle. He gave her an odd look, too.

"There was more to it than that," Jillian said unsteadily.

"Yes, I wanted to marry you, I can't imagine why, you little prude," he said with contempt. "Put a man in prison for trying to teach you about life."

She flushed. She had a good comeback for that, but it was too embarrassing to talk about it in public, especially around men she didn't really know. She felt sick all over.

He came up to her, right up to her, and looked down at her flushed face. "I'm going to be in town for a while, Jillian," he said. "And don't get any ideas about having your boyfriend try to boot me out, or I'll tell him a few things he doesn't know about you."

With that shocking statement, he smiled at the owner, praised the food again and walked out the door.

Jillian sat drinking coffee with cold, trembling hands. She felt the owner's eyes on her, and it wasn't in a way she liked. He seemed to be sizing her up with the new information his customer had given him about her.

People who didn't know you tended to accept even unsavory details with openhandedness, she thought miserably. After all, how well did you really know somebody who worked for you a few days a week? Jillian lived outside town and kept to herself. She wasn't a social person.

There would be gossip, she was afraid, started by the man who'd just gotten out of prison. And how had he gotten out? she wondered. He'd been sentenced to ten years.

When she finished her coffee, she paid for it and left a tip, and paused to speak to the owner. She didn't really know what to say. Her enemy had made an accusation about her, but how did she refute it?

"What he said," she stammered, "there's a lot more to it than it sounds like. I was . . . fifteen."

The owner wasn't a stupid man. He'd known

Jillian since she was a child. "Listen," he said gently, "I don't pay any mind to gossip. I know Jack Haynes, the assistant circuit D.A. He'd never prosecute a man unless he was sure he could get a conviction."

She felt a little relieved. "Thanks, Mr. Chaney."

He smiled. "Don't worry about it. You might talk to Jack, though."

"Yes, I might." She hesitated. "You won't, well, fire me?"

"Don't be ridiculous. And you be careful out there in the snow. If it gets worse, stay home. I can get old Mrs. Barry to sub for you in the morning, okay?"

"Okay," she said. "Thanks."

"We don't want to lose you in an accident," he replied.

She smiled back.

Jack Haynes had his office in the county courthouse, in Hollister. She walked in, hesitantly, and asked the clerk if he was there and could she see him.

"Sure," he said. "He's just going over case files." He grimaced. "Not a fun thing to do. Court's next week."

"I can imagine."

He announced her and she walked in. Jack Haynes smiled, shook hands with her and offered her a chair.

“Davy Harris is out of prison,” she blurted out. “I walked right into him at the restaurant this morning.”

He scowled. “Who’s out?”

She repeated the man’s name.

He pushed the intercom button. “Did we receive notification that they’d released Davy Harris in that attempted rape case?”

“Just a minute, sir, I’ll check.”

The prosecutor cursed under his breath. “I had no idea! You saw him?”

She nodded. “He told everybody in earshot that I had him put in prison for trying to kiss me.” She flushed.

“What a whitewash job!”

“Tell me about it.”

The intercom blared. “Sir, they sent a notification, but it wasn’t on the server. I’m sorry. I don’t know how it got lost.”

“Electronic mail,” Haynes scoffed. “In my day, we went to the post office to get mail!”

“And even there it gets lost sometimes, sir,” his clerk said soothingly. “Sorry.”

“So am I. How did Harris get out?”

“On a technicality, pertaining to the judge’s instructions to the jury being prejudicial to his case,” came the reply. “He’s only out until the retrial.”

“Yes, well, that could take a year or two,” Haynes said coldly.

"Yes," his clerk said quietly.

"Thanks, Chet," he replied, and closed the circuit.

He turned his attention back to Jillian. "That's the second piece of unsettling news I've had from the court system this week," he said curtly. "They've released Smitty Jones, the bank robber, who threatened our police chief, also on a technicality. He's out pending retrial, too." His face hardened. "It shouldn't come as a surprise that they have the same lawyer, some hotshot from Denver."

Jillian clenched her teeth. "He said he'd kill Ted."

Haynes smiled reassuringly. "Better men than him have tried to kill Ted," he pointed out. "He's got good instincts and he's a veteran law enforcement officer. He can take care of himself, believe me."

"I know that, but anybody can be ambushed. Look at Chief Barnes. He was a cautious, capable law enforcement officer, too."

He grimaced. "I knew him. He was such a good man. Shame, what happened."

"Yes."

He gave her a long look. "Jillian, we can't do anything about Harris while he's out on bond," he told her. "But you can take precautions, and you should. Don't go anywhere alone."

"I live alone," she pointed out, worriedly.

He drew in a sharp breath. He'd seen cases like this before, where stalkers had vowed revenge and killed or raped their accusers when they were released from prison. He hated the thought of having something bad happen to this poor woman, who'd seen more than her share of the dark side of men.

"I'll tell Ted," she said after a minute.

His eyebrows arched.

She averted her eyes. "We're sort of in a situation, about the ranch. Our uncles left a clause that if we don't get married, the ranch has to be sold at public auction. Ted thinks we should get married very soon. But I've been hesitant," she said, and bit off the reason.

He knew, without being told by her. "You need to be in therapy," he said bluntly.

She grimaced. "I know. But I can't, I just can't talk about things like that to a stranger."

He had a daughter about her age. He thought how it would be for her in a similar circumstance. It made him sad.

"They're used to all sorts of terrible stories," he began.

"I can't talk about personal things to a stranger," she repeated.

He sighed. "It could ruin your whole life, lock you up in ways you don't even realize yet," he said gently. "I've seen cases where women were never able to marry because of it."

She nodded.

"Don't you want a husband and a family?"

"Very much," she said. She ground her teeth together. "But it seems just hopeless right now." She looked up. "That California developer is licking his lips over my ranch already. But I don't know if I can be a good wife. Ted thinks so, but it's a terrible gamble. I know I have hang-ups."

"They'll get worse," he said bluntly. "I speak from experience. I've tried many cases like yours over the years. I've seen the victims. I know the prognosis. It isn't pretty."

Her eyes were haunted and sad. "I don't understand why he did it," she began.

"It's a compulsion," he explained. "They know it's wrong, but they can't stop. It isn't a matter of will." He leaned forward. "It's like addiction. You know, when men try to give up alcohol, but there's something inside them that pushes them to start drinking again. It doesn't excuse it," he said immediately. "But I'm told that even when they try to live a normal life, it's very difficult. It's one day at a time."

He shook his head. "I see the results of addiction all the time. Alcohol, sex, cards, you name it. People destroy not only their own lives, but the lives of their families because they have a compulsion they can't control."

"It's a shame there isn't a drug you can give

people to keep them from getting addicted," she said absently.

He burst out laughing. "Listen to you. A drug. Drugs are our biggest headache."

She flushed. "Sorry. Wasn't thinking."

He gave her a compassionate smile. "Talk to Ted," he said. "He'll look out for you until our unwanted visitor leaves. In fact, there's a vagrancy law on the books that could give him a reason to make the man leave. Tell him I said so."

She smiled. "I will. Thanks so much, Mr. Haynes."

She stood up. He did, too, and shook her hand.

"If you need help, and you can't find Ted, you can call me," he said unexpectedly. He pulled out a business card and handed it to her. "My Jessica is just your age," he added quietly. "Nothing like that ever happened to her. But if it had, I'd have a hard time remembering that my job is to uphold the law."

"Jessica is very nice."

"Why, thank you," he chuckled. "I think so, too."

They didn't discuss why he'd raised Jessica alone. Her mother had run off with a visiting public-relations man from Nevada and divorced Mr. Haynes. He'd been left with an infant daughter that his wife had no room for in her new and exciting life of travel and adventure. But he'd done very well raising her. Jessica was in medical school, studying to be a doctor. He was very proud of her.

"Don't forget," he told Jillian on the way out. "If you need me, you call."

She was very touched. "Thanks, Mr. Haynes."

He shrugged. "When I'm not working, which isn't often even after hours, my social life is playing World of Warcraft online." He smiled. "I don't get out much. You won't bother me if you call."

"I'll remember."

She went out and closed the door, smiling at the young clerk on her way outside.

She ran headlong into Ted, who had bounded up the steps, wearing an expression that would have stopped a charging bull.

"What did he say to you?" he demanded hotly. His black eyes were sparking with temper.

"What . . . Mr. Haynes?" she stammered, nodding toward the office she'd just left.

"Not him. That . . ." He used some language that lifted both her eyebrows. "Sorry," he said abruptly. "I heard what happened."

She let out a breath. "He announced in the diner that he got put in prison because he wanted to marry me and I didn't want him to kiss me," she said coldly. "He's out on bond because of a technicality, Mr. Haynes said."

"I know. I phoned the prison board."

She tried to smile. "Mr. Haynes says you can arrest him for vagrancy if he stays in town long enough."

He didn't smile back. "He got a job," he said angrily.

She had to lean against the wall for support. "What?"

"He got a damned job in town!" he snapped. "Old Harrington at the feed store hired him on as a day laborer, delivering supplies to ranchers."

She felt sick to her stomach. It meant that Davy Harris had no plans to leave soon. He was going to stay. He was going to live in her town, be around all the time, gossip about her to anybody who would listen. She felt hunted.

Ted saw that and grimaced. He drew her into his arms and held her gently, without passion. "I'll find a way to get him out of here," he said into her hair.

"You can't break the law," she said miserably. She closed her eyes and felt the strong beat of his heart under her ear. "It gets worse. Smitty Jones, that man you arrested for bank robbery, got out, too, didn't he?"

He hesitated. "Yes."

"I guess it's our day for bad news, Ted," she groaned.

He hugged her, hard, and then let her go. "I don't like the idea of your living alone out at the ranch," he said curtly. "It makes you a better target if he came here with plans for revenge. Which he might have."

She bit her lower lip. "I don't want to get married yet."

He let out an exasperated sigh. “I don’t have funds that I could use to get you police protection,” he said angrily. “And even if I did, the man hasn’t made any threats. He’s just here.”

“I know,” she said. “And he’s got a job, you said.”

He nodded. “I could have a word with the owner of the feed store, but that would be crossing the line, big time. I can’t tell a merchant who to hire, as much as I’d like to,” he added.

“I know that. He’d just find another job, anyway, if he’s determined to stay here.” She closed her eyes on a grimace. “He’ll talk to everybody he meets, he’ll say I had him put away for some frivolous reason.” She opened her eyes. “Ted, he makes it all sound like I was just a prude that he shocked with a marriage proposal. He can tell a lie and make it believeable.”

“Some people will believe anything they hear,” he agreed. His black eyes were turbulent. “I don’t like it.”

“I don’t, either.” She felt sick all over. She’d thought things were bad before. Now, they were worse. “I could leave town.”

“That would make it worse,” he said flatly. “If you run, it will give him credibility.”

“I guess so.” She looked up at him worriedly. “Don’t you let him convince you that I had him put away for trying to kiss me. It was a lot more than that.”

He only smiled. "I'm not easy to sway. Besides, I've known you most of your life."

That was true. She didn't add that Ted hadn't known her really well until just recent times.

"There are other people he won't convince, including the prosecutor."

"Mr. Haynes said I could call him if I got in trouble and you weren't available," she said.

He smiled. "He'd come, too. He's a good guy."

"I can't understand why a woman would run away from her husband and a little baby," she said. "He's such a nice person."

"Some women don't want nice, they want dangerous or reckless or vagabond."

"Not me," she said. "I want to stay in Hollister my whole life."

"And have kids?"

She looked up at Ted worriedly. "I want kids a lot," she told him. "It's just . . ."

"It's just what you have to do to make them," he replied.

She blushed.

"Sorry," he said gently. "I didn't mean for it to come out like that."

"I'm a prude. I really am."

"You're not."

She was beginning to wonder. She didn't like recalling what had happened with the man in her past, but his accusations had disturbed her. Was she really so clueless that she'd sent him to prison for something that wasn't his fault? Had she overreacted? She had been at fault with the auditor; she'd gone with him to the motel and at first she'd let him kiss her. Then things got out of hand and she panicked, largely because of what Davy Harris had done to her.

Ted was looking at his watch. "Damn! I've got a meeting with a defense attorney in my office to take a deposition in a theft case. I'll have to go." He bent and kissed her cheek. "You stay clear of that coyote, and if he gives you any trouble, any at all, you tell me. I'll throw his butt in jail."

She smiled. "I will. Thanks, Ted."

"What are friends for?" he asked, and smiled back.

She watched him walk away with misgivings. She wanted to tell him that she wasn't confident about her actions in the past, tell him that maybe the man she'd accused wasn't as guilty as she thought. She wished she had somebody to talk to about it.

She sighed and got in her truck and drove to the ranch. It was going to be the biggest problem of her life, and she didn't know how she was going to solve it.

Things went from bad to worse very quickly. She went in to work the next morning and Davy Harris was sitting in a booth the minute the doors opened. She had to come out to arrange pies and cakes in the display case for the lunch crowd. She didn't work lunch, but she did much of the baking after she'd finished making breakfast for the customers.

Every time she came out to arrange the confections, the man was watching her. He sat as close to the counter as he could get, sipping coffee and giving her malicious looks. He made her very nervous.

"Sir, can I get you anything else?" the waitress, aware of Jillian's discomfort, asked the man in a polite but firm tone.

He lifted his eyebrows. "I'm finishing my coffee."

"Breakfast is no longer being served, sir. We're getting ready for the lunch crowd."

"I know. I'll be back for lunch," he assured her. "I'm almost done."

"Yes, sir." She produced the check and put it next to his plate, and went back to her other customer, the only other one left in the room.

"You always did cook sweets so well, Jilly," Harris told her with a long visual appraisal. "I loved the lemon cake you used to make for your uncle."

"Thanks," she muttered under her breath.

"You live all alone in that big ranch house, now, don't you?" he asked in a pleasant tone that was only surface. His eyes were full of hate. "Don't you get scared at night?"

"I have a shotgun," she blurted out.

He looked shocked. “Really!”

“Really,” she replied with a cold glare. “It would be so unwise for anybody to try to break in at night.”

He laughed coldly. “Why, Jilly, was that a threat?” he asked, raising his voice when the waitress came back to that side of the restaurant. “Were you threatening to shoot me?”

“I was saying that if anybody broke into my house, I would use my shotgun,” she faltered.

“Are you accusing me of trying to break in on you?” he asked loudly.

She flushed. “I didn’t say that.”

“Are you sure? I mean, accusing people of crimes they haven’t committed, isn’t that a felony?” he persisted.

The waitress marched back to his table. “Are you finished, sir?” she asked with a bite in her voice, because she was fond of Jillian. “We have to clear the tables now.”

He sighed. “I guess I’m finished.” He looked at the bill, pulled out his wallet, left the amount plus a ten-cent tip. He gave the waitress an amused smile. “Now, don’t you spend that whole tip all in one place,” he said with dripping sarcasm.

“I’ll buy feed for my polo ponies with it,” she quipped back.

He glared at her. He didn’t like people one-upping him, and it showed. “I’ll see you again, soon, Jilly,” he purred, with a last glance.

He left. Jillian felt her muscles unlocking. But tears stung her eyes.

"Oh, Jill," the waitress, Sandra, groaned. She put her arms around Jillian and hugged her tight. "He'll go away," she said. "He'll have to, eventually. You mustn't cry!"

Jillian bawled. She hadn't known the waitress well at all, until now.

"There, there," Sandra said softly. "I know how it is. I was living with this guy, Carl, and he knocked me around every time he got drunk. Once, he hit me with a glass and it shattered and cut my face real bad. I loved him so much," she groaned. "But that woke me up, when that happened. I moved out. He made threats and even tried to set fire to my house. But when he finally realized I meant it, he gave up and found another girlfriend. Last I heard, she was making weekly trips to the emergency room up in Billings."

Jillian pulled back, wiping her eyes. "It wasn't like that," she whispered. "I was fifteen, and he tried to . . ."

"Fifteen?"

Jillian bit her lower lip. "My uncle hired him as a handy man."

"Good Lord! You should have had him arrested!"

"I did," Jillian said miserably. "But he got out, and now he's going to make my life hell."

"You poor kid! You tell Chief Graves," she said firmly. "He'll take care of it."

Jillian's eyes were misty. "You can't have somebody thrown out of town without good reason," she said. "He hasn't threatened me or done anything except show up here to eat all the time. And it's the only restaurant in town, Sandra," she added.

"Yes, but he was making some pretty thick accusations," she reminded the other girl.

"Words. Just words."

"They can hurt as bad as fists," Sandra said curtly. "I ought to know. My father never hesitated to tell me how ugly and stupid I was."

Jillian gasped. Nobody in her family had ever said such things to her.

"I guess you had nice people to live with, huh?" Sandra asked with a worldly smile. "That wasn't the case with me. My father hated me, because I wasn't his. My mother had an affair. People do it all the time these days. She came back, but he could never get over the fact that she had me by somebody else. She died and he made me pay for it."

"I'm so sorry."

"You're a nice kid," Sandra told her quietly. "That guy makes any trouble for you in here, he'll have to deal with me."

Jillian chuckled. "I've seen you handle unruly customers. You're good at it."

"I ought to be. I was in the army until two years ago," she added. "I worked as military police. Not much I don't know about hand-to-hand combat."

Jillian beamed. "My heroine!"

Sandra just laughed. "Anyway, you get those cakes arranged and go home. I'll deal with the visiting problem while you're away."

"Thanks. For everything."

"Always wished I had a kid sister," Sandra scoffed. She grinned. "So now I do. You tell people I'm your sister and we'll have some laughs."

That would have been funny, because Sandra's skin was a very dark copper, compared to Jillian's very pale skin. Sandra was, after all, full-blooded Lakota.

"Chief Graves is Cheyenne," she said aloud.

"Nothing wrong with the Cheyenne, now that we're not bashing each other's brains out like we did a century ago," came the amused reply. Sandra winked. "Better get cracking. The boss is giving us dark looks."

Jillian grinned. "Can't have that!" she laughed.

Jillian did feel better, and now she had an ally at work. But she was still worried. That man had obviously come to Hollister to pay her back for his jail sentence, and now she was doubting her own story that had cost him his freedom.

Chapter 7

Jillian had never considered that she might become a victim of a stalker. And she wondered if it could even be called stalking. Davy Harris came into the restaurant every morning to eat. But it was the only diner in town. So was that stalking?

Ted thought so, but the law wasn't on the victim's side in this case. A man couldn't be arrested for stalking by eating in the only restaurant in town.

But he made Jillian uptight. She fumbled a cake onto the floor two mornings later, one that had taken a lot of trouble to bake, with cream filling. Harris laughed coldly.

"Why, Jilly, do I make you nervous?" he chided. "I'm only having breakfast here. I haven't tried to touch you or anything."

She cleaned the floor, flushed and unsettled. Sandra had called in sick that morning, so they had a substitute waitress, one who just did her job and didn't waste time on getting to know the other employees. She had no one to back her up, now.

"I only wanted to marry you," Harris said in a soft, quiet tone. "You were real young, but I thought you were mature enough to handle it. And you liked me. Remember when the little white kittens were born and they were going to have to be put down because you couldn't keep them all? I went around to almost every house in town until I found places for them to live."

She bit her lip. That was true. He'd been kind.

"And when your uncle John had that virus and was so sick that he couldn't keep the medicine down? I drove both of you to the hospital."

"Yes," she said reluctantly.

He laughed. "And you repaid my kindness by having me put in prison with murderers."

Her face was stricken as she stared at him.

He got to his feet, still smiling, but his eyes were like a cobra's. "Did you think I'd just go away and you'd never have to see me again?"

She got up, a little wobbly. "I didn't realize . . ."

"What, that I really would go to prison because you exaggerated what happened?" he interrupted. "What kind of woman does that to a man?"

She felt really sick. She knew her face was white.

"I just wanted to marry you and take care of you, and your uncle," he said. "I wouldn't have hurt you. Did I ever hurt you, Jilly?"

She was growing less confident by the second. Had she misjudged him? Was he in prison because she'd blown things out of proportion?

He put a five-dollar bill down beside his plate. "Why don't you think about that?" he continued. "Think about what you did to me. You don't know what it's like in prison, Jilly. You don't know what men can do to other men, especially if they aren't strong and powerful." His face was taut with distaste. "You stupid little prude," he said harshly. "You landed me in hell!"

"I'm . . . I'm sorry," she stammered.

"Are you really?" he asked sarcastically. "Well, not sorry enough, not yet." He leaned toward her. "But you're going to be," he said in a voice that didn't carry. "You're going to wish you never heard my name when I'm through with you."

He stood back up again, smiling like a used car salesman. "It was a really good breakfast, Jilly," he said out loud. "You're still a great little cook. Have a nice day, now."

He walked out, while the owner of the restaurant and the cashier gave him a thoughtful look. Jillian could imagine how it would sound. Here was the poor, falsely accused man trying to be nice to the woman who'd put him away. Jillian wasn't going to come out smelling like roses, no matter what she said or did. And now she had her own doubts about the past. She didn't know what she was going to do.

Ted came by the next day. She heard his car at the front door of the ranch house and she went to the steps with a feeling of unease. She didn't think Ted would take the side of the other man, but Davy could be very convincing.

Ted came up the steps, looking somber. He paused when he saw her expression.

"What's happened?" he asked.

She blinked. "What do you mean?"

"You look like death warmed over."

"Do I? It must be the flour," she lied, and forced a laugh. "I've been making a cherry pie."

Once, he would have made a joke, because it was his favorite. But he was quiet and preoccupied as he followed her into the kitchen.

"Any coffee going?" he asked as he sailed his hat onto the counter.

"I can make some."

"Please."

She started a pot, aware of his keen and penetrating gaze, following her as she worked.

"What's going on with you and Harris?" he asked suddenly.

The question startled her so much that she dropped a pan she'd been putting under the counter. Her hands were shaking.

She turned back to him. "No . . . nothing," she stammered, but her cheeks had flushed.

His face hardened. "Nothing."

"He comes in the restaurant to have breakfast every day," she said.

"And you'd know this, how?"

She put the pan down gently on the counter and drew in a breath. "Because I've got a job there, cooking for the breakfast crowd."

He looked angry. "Since when?"

She hesitated. She hadn't realized how difficult it

was going to be, telling him about her job, and explaining why she'd decided to keep it secret from him. It would look bad, as if she didn't trust him.

The guilt made him angrier.

She poured coffee into a mug and put it in front of him on the table. Her hands were unsteady. "I realize it must seem like I'm keeping secrets," she began.

"It sounds a lot like that."

"I was going to tell you," she protested.

"When?"

She hesitated.

"You said you didn't want to get married yet. Is that why?" he persisted. "You got a job so you could take care of your bills here, so that you could refuse to honor the terms of our uncles' wills?"

It was sounding worse than it was. He was mad. He couldn't even hide it.

He hadn't touched his coffee. He got to his feet. "You back away every time I come close to you. When I take you out, you dress like a teenager going to a dance in the gym. You get a job and don't tell me. You're being overheard flirting with the man who supposedly assaulted you years ago." His eyes narrowed as she searched for ways to explain her behavior. "What other secrets are you keeping from me, Jillian?"

She didn't know what to say that wouldn't make things worse. Her face was a study in misery.

"I'm not flirting with him," she said.

"That isn't what one of the diners said," he returned.

She bit her lower lip. "I've been wondering," she began.

"Wondering what?"

She lifted one shoulder. "Maybe I made a mistake," she blurted out. "Maybe I did exaggerate what happened, because I was so naive." She swallowed hard. "Like with the auditor, when I went out with him and didn't tell him my age, and he got in trouble."

Ted's expression wasn't easily explained. He just stared at her with black eyes that didn't give any quarter at all.

"Davy Harris was kind to Uncle John," she had to admit. "And he was always doing things for him, and for me." She lowered her eyes to the floor, so miserable that she almost choked on her own words. "He said the other men did things to him in prison."

He still hadn't spoken.

She looked up, wincing at his expression. "He wasn't a mean sort of person. He never hurt me . . ."

He picked up his hat, slammed it over his eyes, and walked out the door.

She ran after him. "Ted!"

He kept walking. He went down the steps, got into his truck and drove off without a single word.

Jillian stared after him with a feeling of disaster.

• • •

Sandra gaped at her the next morning at work. "You told Ted Graves that you made a mistake?" she asked. "What in the world is the matter with you? You were so young, Jillian! What sort of man tries to get it on with a kid barely in high school?"

"He was just twenty-one," she protested.

"He should have known better. No jury in the world would have turned him loose for making advances to you."

"Yes, but he, well, while he was in prison, some of the men . . ." She hesitated, searching for the words to explain.

"I know what you mean," Sandra replied shortly. "But you're missing the whole point. A grown man tried to make you go to bed with him when you were young then. Isn't that what happened?"

Jillian drew in a long breath. "Yes. I guess so."

"Then why are you trying to take the blame for it? Did you lead him on? Did you wear suggestive clothing, flirt with him, try to get him to come into your room when your uncle wasn't around?"

"Good heavens, no!" Jillian protested.

Sandra's black eyes narrowed. "Then why is it your fault?"

"He went to prison on my testimony."

"Sounds to me like he deserved to," Sandra replied curtly.

"But he was a kind man," she said. "He was always doing things for other people. One week when Uncle John was real sick, he even did the grocery shopping for us."

"A few years back in a murder trial, a witness testified that the accused murderer helped her take her groceries into the house. Another told the jury that he tuned up her old car when it wouldn't start. What does that have to do with a man's guilt or innocence?"

Jillian blinked. "Excuse me?"

"Don't you think that a man can do kind things and still kill someone, given the motive?" she asked.

"I never thought of it like that."

"Even kind people can kill, Jillian," Sandra said bluntly. "I knew this guy on the reservation, Harry. He'd give you the shirt off his back. He drove old Mr. Hotchkiss to the doctor every month to get his checkup. But he killed another man in an argument and got sent to prison for it. Do you think they should have acquitted him because he did a couple of kind things for other people?"

"Well, no," she had to admit.

"We all have good and evil in us," the older woman replied. "Just because we're capable of good doesn't mean we can't do something evil."

"I guess I understand."

"You think about that. And stop trying to assume responsibility for something that wasn't your fault. You were just out of grade school when it happened. You weren't old enough or mature enough to permit any man liberties like that, at the time. You weren't old enough to know better, Jillian, but he was."

She felt a little better.

"Besides that, did you like it?"

"Are you kidding?" Jillian exclaimed. "No, I hated it!"

"Then that should tell you who's at fault, shouldn't it?"

Jillian began to relax. "You have a way with words."

"I should have been a writer," Sandra agreed. She grinned, showing perfect white teeth. "Now you stop spouting nonsense and start working on that bacon. We'll have customers ranting because breakfast isn't ready!"

Jillian laughed. "I guess we will. Thanks."

Sandra grinned. "You're welcome."

Jillian didn't go out front when the doors opened, not even to put out the cakes and pies. Sandra did that for her.

"Curious," she said when she came back into the kitchen.

"What is?"

"Your old friend Davy wasn't out there."

"Maybe he decided to leave," Jillian said hopefully.

"It would take somebody more gullible than me to believe that," the older woman replied.

"Yes, but I can hope."

"Know what the Arabs say?" Sandra asked. "They say, trust in Allah, but tie up your camel. Sound advice," she added, shaking a long finger at the other woman.

Jillian did hope for the best, anyway, and not only about Davy Harris leaving town. She hoped that Ted might come by to talk, or just smooth things over with her. But he didn't come to the restaurant, or to the ranch. And the next morning, Davy Harris was right back in the same booth, waiting for his breakfast.

"Did you miss me?" he teased Jillian, having surprised her as she was putting a pound cake in the display case.

"I didn't notice you were gone," she lied, flushing.

"We both know better than that, don't we?" He leaned back in the booth, his pale eyes so smug that it made her curious. "I've been talking to people about you."

She felt uneasy. "What people?"

"Just people."

She didn't know what to say. She got to her feet and went back into the kitchen. Her stomach was cutting somersaults all the way.

That afternoon, as she went out to get into her old vehicle to go home, she walked right into Davy.

She gasped and jumped back. He laughed.

"Do I make you nervous?" he chided. "I can't imagine why. You know, I never tried to hurt you. I never did. Did I?"

"N-no," she blurted out, embarrassed, because a few people standing outside the bank were listening, and watching them.

"I told your uncle I wanted to marry you," he said, without lowering his voice. He even smiled. "He said that he hoped I would, because he liked me and he knew I'd take care of you. But that was before you told those lies about me, wasn't it, Jilly? That was before you got me put in jail for trying to kiss you."

She was embarrassed because they were talking about something private in a very public location, and several people were listening.

"It wasn't . . . wasn't like that," she stammered, flushing.

"Yes, it was, you just don't like admitting that you made a mistake," he said, his voice a little louder now. "Isn't that the truth?"

She was fumbling for words. She couldn't get her mind to work at all.

"You lied about me," he continued, raising his voice. "You lied."

She should have disputed that. She should have said that it was no lie, that he'd tried to assault her in her own home. But she was too embarrassed. She turned and almost ran to her truck. Once inside, she locked the door with cold, trembling fingers.

Davy stood on the sidewalk, smiling. Just smiling. A man and woman came up to him and he turned and started talking to them as Jillian drove away. She wondered what they were saying. She hoped it wasn't about her.

But in the next few days, she noticed a change in attitude, especially in customers who came to the restaurants. Her pretty cakes had been quickly bought before, but now they stayed in the case. Jill took most of them back home. When she went to the bank, the teller was polite, but not chatty and friendly as she usually was.

Even at the local convenience store where she bought gas, the clerk was reserved, all business, when she paid at the counter.

The next morning, at work, she began to understand why she was being treated to a cold shoulder from people she'd known most of her life.

"Everybody thinks you did a job on me, Jilly," Davy said under his breath when she was putting a cake on the counter—only one cake today, instead of the variety she usually produced, since they weren't selling.

She glared at him over the cake. "It wouldn't do to tell them the truth."

"What is the truth?" He leaned back in the booth,

his eyes cold and accusing. "You had me sent to jail."

She stood up, tired of being harassed, tired of his unspoken accusations, tired of the way local people were treating her because of him.

"I was a freshman in high school and you tried to force me to have sex with you," she said shortly, aware of a shocked look from a male customer. "How hard is that to understand? It's called statutory rape, I believe . . . ?"

Davy flushed. He got to his feet and towered over her. "I never raped you!"

"You had my clothes off and the only reason you stopped was because I slugged you and ran. If Sassy Peale hadn't had a shotgun, you never would have stopped! You ran after me all the way to her house!"

He clenched his fists by his side. "I went to jail," he snapped. "You're going to pay for that. I'll make sure you pay for that!"

She took the cake, aimed it and threw it right in his face.

"I could have you arrested for assault!" he sputtered.

"Go ahead," she said, glaring at him. "I'll call the police for you, if you like!"

He took a quick step toward her, but the male customer stood up all at once and moved toward him. He backed away.

"You'll be sorry," he told Jillian. He glared at the

other customer, and walked out, wiping away cake with a handkerchief.

Jillian was shaking, but she hadn't backed down. She took a shaky breath, fighting tears, and started picking up cake.

"You think he'll go away," the customer, a tall blond man with a patch over one eye, said quietly, in an accented tone, like a British accent, but with a hard accent on the consonants. She recalled hearing accents like that in one of the *Lethal Weapon* movies. "He won't."

She stopped picking up cake and got to her feet, staring at him.

He was tall and well built. His blond hair was in a ponytail. His face was lean, with faint scars, and he had one light brown eye visible. He looked like the sort of man who smiled a lot, but he wasn't smiling now. He had a dangerous look.

"You should talk to a lawyer," he said quietly.

She bit her lip. "And say what? He eats here every day, but this is the only restaurant in town."

"It's still harassment."

She sighed. "Yes. It is. But I can't make him leave."

"Talk to Ted Graves. He'll make him leave."

"Ted isn't speaking to me."

He lifted an eyebrow expressively.

"I ticked him off, too, by saying I might have made a mistake and overreacted to what Davy did to me," she said miserably. "Davy made it sound as if I did. And then he reminded me about all the kind things he did for my uncle and me . . .”

“Adolph Hitler had a dog. He petted it and took it for walks and threw sticks for it to chase,” he said blandly.

She grimaced. She went back down and picked up more cake.

“If you were so young and it took a shotgun to deter him,” the man continued, “it wasn’t an innocent act.”

“I’m just beginning to get that through my thick skull,” she sighed.

“This sort of man doesn’t quit,” he continued, sticking his hands deep in the pockets of his jeans. His eye was narrow and thoughtful. “He’s here for more than breakfast, if you get my drift. He wants revenge.”

“I guess so.”

“I hope you keep a gun.”

She laughed. “I hate guns.”

“So do I,” he mused. “I much prefer knives.”

He indicated a huge Bowie knife on one hip, in a fringed leather sheath.

She stared at it. “I don’t guess you’d have to do much more than show that to somebody to make them back off.”

“That’s usually the case.”

She finished cleaning up the cake. “They aren’t selling well lately, but I thought this one might. Davy seems to have been spending all his spare time telling people what an evil woman I am. There's a distinct chill in the air wherever I go now."

"That's because he's telling his side of the story to anybody who'll listen," he replied. "And that's harassment, as well."

"I can see Ted arresting him for talking to someone," she said sarcastically.

"It depends on what he's saying. I heard what he said in here. If you need a witness, I'm available."

She frowned. "He didn't say much."

"He said enough," he replied.

She shrugged. "I like to handle my own problems."

"Ordinarily I'd say that's admirable. Not in this case. You're up against a man who's done hard time and came out with a grudge. He wants blood. If you're not very careful, he'll get it. He's doing a number on your character already. People tend to believe what they want to believe, and it isn't always the truth. Especially when a likeable young man who's apparently been railroaded by a nasty young girl tells the right kind of story."

She blinked. "I'd be the nasty young girl in this story?"

He nodded.

She put the remnants of her cake into the trash can behind the counter. She shrugged. "I never thought of myself as a bad person."

"It's his thoughts that you have to worry about.

If he's mad enough, and I think he is if he came here expressly to torment you, he won't stop with gossip."

That thought had occurred to her, too. She looked up at the customer with wide, worried eyes. "Maybe I should get a job over in Billings."

"And run for it?" he asked. "Fat chance. He'd follow you."

She gasped. "No . . . !"

His face hardened. "I've seen this happen before, in a similar case," he said tersely. "In fact, I was acting as an unpaid bodyguard as a favor to a friend. The perp not only got out of jail, he went after the girl who testified against him and beat her up."

She glared. "I hope you hurt him."

"Several of us," he replied, "wanted to, but her boyfriend got to him first. He's back in jail. But if she'd been alone, there might not have been anybody to testify."

She felt sick to her stomach. "You're saying something, aren't you?"

"I'm saying that such men are unpredictable," he replied. "It's better to watch your back than to assume that everything will work itself out. In my experience, situations like this don't get better."

She put down the rag she'd been cleaning with, and looked up with worried eyes. "I wish Ted wasn't mad at me," she said quietly.

"Go make up with him," he advised. "And do it

soon." He didn't add that he'd seen the expression on her assailant's face and he was certain the man would soon resort to violence to pay her back.

"I suppose I should," she said. She managed a smile. "Thanks, Mr. . . . ?"

"Just call me Rourke," he said, and grinned. "Most people do."

"Are you visiting somebody local?"

His eyebrows arched. "Don't I look like a local?"

She shook her head, softening the noncomment with a smile.

He laughed. "Actually," he said, "I came by to see the police chief. And not on a case. Ted and I were in the military together. I brought a message from an old friend who works as a police chief down in Texas."

She cocked her head. "That wouldn't be the one who taught him to tango?"

He blinked his single eye. "He taught Ted to dance?"

She nodded. "He's pretty good, too."

Rourke chuckled. "Wonders never cease."

"That's what I say."

He smiled down at her. "Talk to Ted," he advised. "You're going to need somebody who can back you up, if that man gets violent."

"I'll do that," she said after a minute. "And thanks."

"You're welcome, but for what?"

"For making me see the light," she replied flatly.

"I've been blaming myself for sending Davy to prison."

"You mark my words," he replied. "Very soon, Davy is going to prove to you that it was where he belonged."

She didn't reply. She just hoped it wasn't a prophecy. But she was going to see Ted, the minute she got off work.

Chapter 8

Before Jillian could finish her chores and get out of the restaurant, Sassy Peale Callister came into the restaurant and dragged her to one side.

"I can't believe what I just heard," she said shortly. "Did you actually say that you might have been wrong to have Davy Harris put in jail?"

Jillian flushed to the roots of her hair. "How did you hear about that?" she stammered.

"Hollister is a very small town. You tell one person and everybody else knows," the other woman replied. "Come on, is it true?"

Jillian felt even more uncomfortable. "He was reminding me how much he helped me and Uncle John around the ranch. He was always kind to us. Once, when we were sick, he went to the store and pharmacy for us, and then nursed us until we were well again."

Sassy wasn't buying it. Her face was stony. "That means he's capable of doing good deeds. It doesn't mean he can't do bad things."

"I know," Jillian said miserably. "It's just . . . well, he's been in here every day. He makes it sound like I overreacted . . ."

"You listen to me, he's no heartsick would-be suitor," Sassy said firmly. "He's a card-carrying coyote with delusions of grandeur! I wasn't sure that he wasn't going to try to take the shotgun away from me, even if I'd pulled the trigger. He was furious! Don't you remember what he said?"

Jillian glanced around her. The restaurant was empty, but the owner was nearby, at least within earshot.

"He said that he'd get both of us," Sassy replied. "John thinks he meant it and that he's here for revenge. He hired me a bodyguard, if you can believe that." She indicated the tall man with a long blond ponytail and a patch over one eye.

"That's Rourke," Jilly exclaimed.

Sassy blinked. "Excuse me?"

"That's Rourke. He was in here this morning, when I threw a cake at Davy." She ignored Sassy's gasp and kept going. "He said that I was nuts trying to make excuses for the man, and that I should make up with Ted. He thinks Davy is dangerous."

"So do I," Sassy said quietly. "You should come and stay with us until this is over, one way or the other."

Jillian was tempted. But she thought of little Sammy and a means of revenge that might occur to a mind as twisted as Davy's. He might even burn the house down. She didn't dare leave it unattended.

"Thanks," she said gently, "but I can't do that. Anyway, I've got my uncle's shotgun."

"Which you've never touched," Sassy muttered. "I doubt it's been cleaned since he died."

Jillian stared at the floor. "Ted would clean it for me if I asked him to."

"Why don't you ask him to?" came the short reply. "And then tell him why you need it cleaned. I dare you."

"I don't think Davy would hurt me, really," she said slowly.

"He assaulted you."

"Maybe he just got, well, overstimulated, and . . ."

"He assaulted you," Sassy replied firmly.

Jillian sighed. "I hate unpleasantness."

"Who doesn't? But this isn't just a man who let a kiss go too far. This is a man who deliberately came to Hollister, got a job and devils you every day at your place of work," Sassy said quietly. "It's harassment. It's stalking. Maybe you can't prove it, but you should certainly talk to Ted about it."

"He'll think I'm overreacting."

"He's a policeman," Sassy reminded her. "He won't."

Jillian was weakening. She was beginning to feel even more afraid of Davy. If Sassy's husband thought there was a threat, and went so far as to hire his wife a bodyguard, he must be taking it seriously.

"John tried to have him arrested, but Ted reminded him that you can't put somebody behind bars for something he said years ago. He has to have concrete evidence."

That made things somehow even worse. Jillian's worried eyes met her friend's. "Davy does scare me."

Sassy moved closer. "I'm going to have Rourke keep an eye on you, too, when I'm safely home with John. We've got enough cowboys at the ranch who have federal backgrounds to keep me safe," she added with a chuckle. "One of them used to work for the godfather of John's sister-in-law. He was a mercenary with mob connections. He's got millions and he still comes to see her." She leaned forward, so that Rourke couldn't hear. "There was gossip once that Rourke was his son. Nobody knows and Rourke never talks about him."

"Wow," Jillian exclaimed. "That would be K.C. Kantor, wouldn't it?"

Sassy was impressed. "How did you know?"

"I wouldn't have, but your husband was talking about him at the restaurant one morning when you were on that shopping trip to Los Angeles and he had to eat in town."

"Eavesdropping, were you?" Sassy teased.

Jillian smiled. "Sorry. Sometimes a waitress can't help it."

"I don't mind." She drew in a breath. "I have to go. But if you need anything, you call. I'll lend Rourke to you."

"My ears work, even if I'm missing one eye," the tall blond man drawled.

Both women turned, surprised.

"And K.C. Kantor is not my father." He bit off every word. "That's malicious gossip, aimed at my dad, who was a military man in South Africa and made enemies because of his job."

"Sorry," Sassy said at once, and looked uneasy. Rourke rarely did anything except smile pleasantly and crack jokes, but his pale brown eye was glittering and he looked dangerous.

He saw the consternation his words had produced, and fell back into his easygoing persona with no visible effort. He grinned. "I eavesdrop shamelessly, too," he added. "I never know when some pretty young woman might be making nice remarks about me. Wouldn't want to miss it."

They both relaxed.

"Sorry," Sassy said again. "I wasn't saying it to be unkind."

He shrugged. "I know that. Kantor took me in when I was orphaned, because he and my dad were friends. It's a common misconception." He frowned. "You're right about Jillian. Living alone is dangerous when you've got an enemy with unknown intentions. Mrs. Callister is safe at night, unless she's going out without her husband. I could come over and sleep on your sofa, if you like."

"Yes, he could," Sassy seconded at once.

That made Jillian visibly uncomfortable. She averted her eyes. "That's very kind of you, thanks, but I'll manage."

Rourke lifted an eyebrow. "Is it my shaving

lotion? I mean, it does sometimes put women off," he said blandly.

Sassy laughed. "No. It's convention."

"Excuse me?"

"She won't stay alone at night with a man in the house," Sassy said. "And before you say anything—" she stopped him when he opened his mouth to reply "—I would have felt exactly the same way when I was single. Women in small towns, brought up with certain attitudes, don't entertain single men at night."

He looked perplexed.

"You've never lived in a small town," Jillian ventured.

"I was born in Africa," he said, surprisingly. "I've lived in small villages all my life. But I don't know much about small American towns. I suppose there are similarities. Well, except for the bride price that still exists in some places."

"Bride price?" Jillian stared at him, waiting.

"A man who wants to marry a woman has to give her father a certain number of cattle."

She gaped at him.

"It's a centuries-old tradition," he explained. He pursed his lips and smiled at Jillian. "I'll bet your father would have asked a thousand head for you."

She glared at him. "My father would never have offered to sell me to you!" she exclaimed.

"Different places, different customs," he said

easily. “I’ve lived in places, in ways, that you might never imagine.”

“John said you were a gunrunner,” Sassy mused.

He glared at her. “I was not,” he said indignantly. Then he grinned. “I was an arms dealer.”

“Semantics!” she shot back.

He shrugged again. “A man has to make a living when he’s between jobs. At the time, there wasn’t much action going on in my part of Africa for mercenaries.”

“And now you work as a bodyguard?” Jillian asked.

He hesitated. “At times, when I’m on vacation. I actually work as an independent contractor these days. Legit,” he added when they looked at him with open suspicion. “I don’t do mercenary work anymore.”

“So that case in Oklahoma where you helped free a kidnapping victim was legit, too?” Sassy asked.

“I was helping out a friend,” he replied, chuckling. “He works for the same federal agency I work for these days.”

“But you’re an African citizen, aren’t you?” Jillian asked. “I mean, if you were born there . . . ?”

“I have American citizenship now,” he said, and looked uncomfortable.

“When he went to work for Mr. Kantor, he had to have it,” Sassy murmured. “I imagine he pulled some strings at the state department?”

Rourke just looked at her, without speaking.

She held out her hands, palms up. "Okay, I'm sorry, I won't pry. I'm just grateful you're around to look out for me." She glanced at Jillian. "But you still have a problem. What if Harris decides he wants to get even one dark night, and you can't get to that shotgun in time? The one that hasn't been cleaned since your uncle died?"

"I said I'd get Ted to clean it for me," the other woman protested.

"You and Ted aren't speaking."

"I'll come over and clean it for you," Rourke said quietly. "And teach you to shoot it."

Jillian looked hunted. "I hate guns," she burst out. "I hated it when Ted would come over and shoot targets from the front porch. I'll never get used to the sound of them. It's like dynamite going off in my ears!"

Rourke looked at her with shocked disdain. "Didn't anybody ever tell you about earplugs?"

"Earplugs?"

"Yes. You always wear them on the gun range," he explained, "unless you want to go deaf at an early age. Ear protectors are fine on the range, but earplugs can be inserted quickly if you're on a job and expecting trouble."

"How do you hear?"

"They let in sound. They just deaden certain frequencies of sound," he explained. He glanced at Sassy. "You won't need me tonight. I heard your husband say he's lined up a new werewolf movie to watch with you on pay-per-view."

She laughed. "Yes. It's the second in a vampire trilogy, actually. I love it!"

He didn't react. He glanced toward Jillian. "So I'll be free about six. I can come over and clean the shotgun and do a security sweep. If you need locks and silent sentries, I can install them."

She bit her lip, hard. She couldn't afford such things. She could barely pay the bills on what she made as a cook.

The owner of the restaurant, who had been blatantly eavesdropping, joined them. "You can have an advance on your salary anytime you need it," he told Jillian gently. "I'd bar Harris from coming on the premises, if I could, but he's the sort who'd file a lawsuit. I can't afford that," he added heavily.

"Thanks, Mr. Chaney," Jillian said quietly. "I thought you might fire me, because of all that's going on right now."

"Fat chance," he said amusedly. "You're the best cook I've ever had."

"He shouldn't be allowed to harass her while she's doing her job," Sassy said curtly.

"I agree," the restaurant owner said gently. "But this is a business and I can't bar people I dislike without proof they're causing problems. I've never heard him threaten Jillian or even be disrespectful to her."

"That's because he whispers things to me that he doesn't want anybody to overhear," she said miserably. "He made me believe that I had him locked up for no reason at all."

"I live in Hollister," he said quietly. "Even if it's not in blaring headlines, most of us know what's going on here. I remember the case. My sister, if you recall, was the assistant prosecutor in the case. She helped Jack Haynes with the precedents."

"I do remember," Jillian said. She folded her arms over her slight breasts. "It's so scary. I never thought he'd get out."

"People get out all the time on technicalities," Rourke said. "A case in point is the bank robber your police chief put away. And a friend of mine in the FBI in Texas has a similar problem. A man he sent away for life just got out and is after him. My friend can't do much more than you're doing. The stalker doesn't do anything he could even be charged with."

"Life is hard," Sassy said.

"Then you die," Rourke quipped, and grinned. "Did you watch that British cop show, too? You're pretty young."

"Everything's on disc now, even those old shows. It's one of John's favorites," Sassy chuckled.

"Mine, too," Chaney added, laughing. "They were an odd mix, the female British cop and the American one, in a team."

"Pity it ended before we knew how things worked out between them," Rourke sighed. "I would have loved a big, romantic finale."

Both women and the restaurant owner stared at him.

"I'm a romantic," he said defensively.

The women stared pointedly at the pistol in the shoulder holster under his loose jacket.

"I can shoot people and still be romantic," he said belligerently. "Out there somewhere is a woman who can't wait to marry me and have my children!"

They stared more.

He moved uncomfortably. "Well, my profession isn't conducive to child-raising, I guess, but I could still get married to some nice lady who wanted to cook and darn my socks and take my clothes to the dry cleaner when I was home between jobs."

"That's not romantic, that's delusional," Sassy told him.

"And you're living in the wrong century," Jillian added.

He glared. "I'm not shacking up with some corporate raider in a pin-striped business suit."

"It's not called shacking up, it's called cohabiting," Sassy said drolly. "And I really can't see you with a corporate raider. I should think a Dallas Cowboy linebacker would be . . . Don't hit me, I'll tell John!" she said in mock fear when he glowered and took a step forward.

“A woman in a pin-striped suit,” he qualified.

Sassy nodded. “A female mob hit-person.”

He threw up his hands. “I can’t talk to you.”

“You could if you’d stop mixing metaphors and looking for women who lived in the dark ages.” She frowned. “You don’t get out much, do you?”

He looked out the window of the restaurant. “In this burg, it wouldn’t matter if I did. I think there are two unmarried ladies who live in this town, and they’re both in their sixties!”

“We could ask if anybody has pretty cousins or nieces who live out of town,” Jillian offered.

He gave her a pursed-lip scrutiny. “You’re not bad. You have your own ranch and you can cook.”

“I don’t want to get married,” Jillian said curtly.

“That’s true,” Sassy said sadly. “I think Harris has put her off men for life. She won’t even marry Ted, and that means she’ll lose the ranch to a developer.”

“Good grief,” Rourke exclaimed. “Why?”

“It’s in my uncle’s will and his uncle’s will that we have to marry each other or the ranch gets sold at public auction,” Jillian said miserably. “There’s a California developer licking his lips in the background, just waiting to turn my ranch into a resort.”

Rourke was outraged. “Not that beautiful hunk of land!”

She nodded. “It will look like the West Coast

when he gets through. He'll cut down all the trees, pave the land, and build expensive condominiums. I hear he even has plans for a strip mall in the middle. Oh, and an amusement park."

Rourke was unusually thoughtful. "Nice piece of land, that," he remarked.

"Very nice."

"But that doesn't solve your problem," Sassy replied.

"I can be over about six, if that's okay?" he told Jillian, with a questioning glance at Sassy.

"That will be fine with us," Sassy assured him. She glared at Jillian, who was hesitating. "If Ted won't talk to you, somebody has to clean the shotgun."

"I suppose so."

"Enthusiasm like that has launched colonies," Rourke drawled.

Jillian laughed self-consciously. "Sorry. I don't mean to sound reluctant. I just don't know what Ted will think. He's already mad because I said I might have overreacted to Davy Harris when I had him arrested."

"It wasn't overreaction," the restaurant owner, Mr. Chaney, inserted indignantly. "The man deserved what he got. I'm just sorry I can't keep him out of here. If he ever insults you or makes a threat, you tell me. I'll bar him even if I do get sued."

"Thanks, boss. Really," Jillian said.

"Least I could do." He glanced at the front door. "Excuse me. Customers." He left with a smile.

"He always greets people when they come in," Jillian explained with a smile, "and then he comes around to the tables and checks to make sure the service and the food are okay with them. He's a great boss."

"It's a good restaurant," Rourke agreed. "Good food." He grinned at Jillian.

"So. Six?" he added.

Jillian smiled. "Six. I'll even feed you."

"I'll bring the raw materials, shall I?" he asked with a twinkle in his eyes. "Steaks and salad?"

"Lovely!" Jillian exclaimed. "I haven't had a steak in a long time!"

"You've got all that beef over there and you don't eat steak?" he exclaimed. "What about that prime young calf, the little steer . . . ?"

"Sammy?" Jillian gasped. "She's not eating beef!"

"She?" he asked.

"She's a cow. Or she will be one day."

"A cow named Sammy." He laughed. "Sounds like Cy Parks, down in Jacobsville, Texas. He's got a girl dog named Bob."

Everyone laughed.

"See?" Jillian said indignantly. "I'm not the only person who comes up with odd names for animals."

Sassy hugged her. “No, you aren’t. I’m going home. You let Rourke clean that shotgun.”

“Okay. Thanks,” she added.

“My pleasure,” Rourke said.

Sassy grinned. “And don’t let him talk you into marrying him,” she added firmly. “Ted will never speak to us again.”

“No danger of that,” Jillian sighed. “Sorry,” she added to Rourke.

“Don’t be so hasty, now,” Rourke said. “I have many good qualities. I’ll elaborate on them tonight. See you at six.”

He left with Sassy. Jillian stared after them, grateful but uneasy. What was Ted going to think?

Rourke showed up promptly at six with a bag of groceries.

He put his purchases out on the table. Expensive steaks, lettuce, all the ingredients for salad plus a variety of dressings, and a cherry pie and a pint of vanilla ice cream.

“I know you cook pies and cakes very well,” he explained, “but I thought you might like a taste of someone else’s cooking. Mrs. Callister’s new cook produced that. It’s famous where she comes from, up in Billings, Montana.”

“I’ll love it. Cherry pie is one of my favorites.”

“Mine, too.”

He started the steaks and then used her gourmet

knives to do a fantastic chopping of vegetables for the salad.

Jillian watched his mastery of knives with pure fascination. "It must have taken you a long time to learn to do that so effortlessly."

"It did. I practiced on many people."

She stared at him, uncertain how to react.

He saw that and burst out laughing. "I was joking," he explained. "Not that I've never used knives on people, when the occasion called for it."

"I suppose violence is a way of life to someone in your position."

He nodded. "I learned to handle an AK-47 when I was ten years old."

She gasped.

"Where I grew up, in Africa, there were always regional wars," he told her. "The musclemen tried to move in and take over what belonged to the local tribes. I didn't have family at that time, was living in an orphanage, so I went to fight with them." He laughed. "It was an introduction to mean living that I've never been able to get past. Violence is familiar."

"I suppose it would have to be."

"I learned tactics and strategy from a succession of local warlords," he told her. "Some of them were handed down from the time of Shaka Zulu himself."

"Who was that?"

"Shaka Zulu? The most famous of the Zulu

warriors, a strategist of the finest kind. He revolutionized weaponry and fighting styles among his people and became a great warlord. He defeated the British, with their advanced weapons."

"Good grief! I never heard of him."

"There was a miniseries on television about his exploits," he said while he chopped celery and cucumbers into strips. "I have it. I watch it a lot."

"I saw *Out of Africa.*"

He smiled. "That's a beaut."

"It is. I loved the scenery." She laughed. "Imagine, playing Mozart for the local apes."

"Inventive." He stopped chopping, and his eye became dreamy. "I think Africa is the most beautiful place on earth. It's sad that the animals are losing habitat so quickly. Many of the larger ones will go extinct in my lifetime."

"There are lots of people trying to save them. They raise the little ones and then turn them back out onto the land."

"Where poachers are waiting to kill them," he said laconically. "You can still find ivory, and elephant feet used for footstools, and rhinoceros horn in clandestine shops all over the world. They do catch some of the perps, but not all of them. It's tragic to see a way of life going dead. Like the little Bushmen," he added quietly. "Their culture was totally destroyed, denigrated, ridiculed as worthless by European invaders. The end result is that they became displaced people, living in cities, in slums. Many are alcoholics."

"I could tell you the same is true here, where Native Americans received similar treatment," she told him.

He smiled. "It seems that the old cultures are so primitive that they're considered without value. Our greatest modern civilizations are less than two thousand years old, yet those of primitive peoples can measure in the hundreds of thousands. Did you know that the mighty civilizations of Middle America were based on agriculture? Ours are based on industry."

"Agriculture. Farming."

He nodded. "Cities grew up around irrigated lands where crops were planted and grew even in conditions of great drought. The Hohokam in Arizona had canals. The Mayan civilization had astronomy." He glanced at her. "The medical practitioners among the Incas knew how to do trepanning on skulls to relieve pressure in the brain. They used obsidian scalpels. It isn't well-known, but they're still in use today in scalpels for surgery."

"How did you learn all that?" she wondered.

"Traveling. It's one of the perks of my job. I get to see things and mix with people who are out in the vanguard of research and exploration. I once acted as bodyguard to one of the foremost archaeologists on earth in Egypt."

"Gosh!"

"Have you ever traveled?" he asked.

She thought about that. "Well, I did go to Oklahoma City, once," she said. "It was a long drive."

He was holding the knife in midair. "To Oklahoma City."

She flushed. "It's the only place outside Montana that I've ever been," she explained.

He was shocked. "Never to another country?"

"Oh, no," she replied. "There was never enough money for . . ." She stopped and glanced out the window. A pickup truck pulled up in the yard, very fast. The engine stopped, the door opened and was slammed with some fury.

Rourke's hand went involuntarily to the pistol under his arm.

"Oh, dear," Jillian said, biting her lip.

"Harris?" he asked curtly.

She sighed. "Worse. It's Ted."

Chapter 9

There were quick, heavy footsteps coming up onto the porch. Jillian didn't have to ask if Ted was mad. When he wasn't, his tread was hardly audible at all, even in boots. Now, he was walking with a purpose, and she could hear it.

He knocked on the door. She opened it and stepped back.

His black eyes glittered at her. "I hear you have company," he said shortly.

Rourke came out of the kitchen. His jacket was off, so the .45 automatic he carried was plainly visible in its holster. "She does, indeed," he replied. He moved forward with easy grace and extended a hand. "Rourke," he introduced himself. "I'm on loan from the Callisters."

Ted shook the hand. "Theodore Graves. Chief of police," he added.

Rourke grinned. "I knew that. I came to town to try to see you the other day, but you were out on a case. Cash Grier said to tell you hello."

Ted seemed surprised. "You know him?"

"We used to work together under, shall we say, unusual conditions, in Africa," came the reply.

Ted relaxed a little. "Rourke. I think he mentioned you."

He shrugged. "I get around. I really came over to clean her shotgun for her, but I'm cooking, too."

He gave Ted an appraisal that didn't miss much, including the other man's jealousy. "I'm impressing her with my culinary skills, in hopes that she might want to marry me after supper."

Ted gaped at him. "What?"

"He's just kidding," Jillian said, flushing.

"I am?" Rourke asked, and raised both eyebrows.

Ted glared at the other man. "She's engaged to me."

"I am not!" Jillian told him emphatically.

Rourke backed up a step and held up a hand. "I think I'll go back into the kitchen. I don't like to get mixed up in family squabbles," he added with a grin.

"We are not a family, and we're not squabbling!" Jillian raged.

"We're going to be a family, and yes, we are," Ted said angrily.

Rourke discreetly moved into the kitchen.

"I could have cleaned the shotgun, if you'd just asked me," he said angrily.

"You stormed out of here in a snit and never said a word," she returned. "How was I supposed to ask you, mail a letter?"

"Email is quicker," came a droll voice from the kitchen.

"You can shut up, this is a private argument," Ted called back.

"Sorry," Rourke murmured. "Don't be too long now, cold steak is unappetizing."

"You're feeding him steak?" Ted exclaimed. "What did he do, carve up Sammy?"

"I don't eat ugly calves!" Rourke quipped.

"Sammy is not ugly, she's beautiful!" Jillian retorted.

"If you say so," Rourke said under his breath.

"There's nothing wrong with black baldies," she persisted.

"Unless you've never seen a Brahma calf," Rourke sighed. "Gorgeous little creatures."

"Brahmas are the ugliest cattle on earth," Ted muttered.

"They are not!" Rourke retorted. "I own some of them!"

Ted stopped. "You run cattle around here?" he asked.

Rourke came back into the room, holding a fork. "In Africa. My home is in Kenya."

Ted's eyes narrowed. "So that's how Cash met you."

"Yes. I was, shall we say, gainfully employed in helping oust a local warlord who was slaughtering children in his rush to power."

"Good for you," Ted replied.

"Now you're teaming up?" Jillian said, fuming.

"Only as far as cattle are concerned," Rourke assured her with a flash of white teeth. "I'm still a contender in the matrimonial sweepstakes," he added. "I can cook and clean and make apple strudel." He gave Ted a musing appraisal, as if to say, top that.

Ted was outdone. It was well-known that he couldn't boil water. He glared at the blond man. "I can knock pennies off bottles with my pistol," he said, searching for a skill to compare.

"I can do it with an Uzi," Rourke replied.

"Not in my town, you won't—that's an illegal weapon."

"Okay, but that's a sad way to cop out of a competition." He blinked. "I made a pun!"

"I'm not a cop, I'm a police chief."

"Semantics," Rourke said haughtily, borrowing Jillian's favorite word, and walked back to the kitchen.

Ted looked down at Jillian, who was struggling not to laugh. He was more worried than he wanted to admit about her assailant, who kept adding fuel to the fire in town with gossip about Jillian's past. He knew better, but some people wouldn't. He'd been irritable because he couldn't find a way to make the little weasel leave town. Jillian was pale and nervous. He hadn't helped by avoiding her. It was self-defense. She meant more to him than he'd realized. He didn't want her hurt, even if she couldn't deal with marrying him.

He rested his hand on the butt of the automatic holstered on his belt. "I heard about what happened in the restaurant. You should listen to

Sassy. It's possible that Harris may try to get revenge on you here, where you're alone."

"She's not alone," Rourke chimed in. "I'm here."

"Not usually, and he'll know that," Ted said irritably. He didn't like the other man assuming what he thought of as his own responsibility.

"Mrs. Callister already asked her to come stay at the ranch, but she won't," came the reply.

Ted didn't like the idea of Jillian being closer to Rourke, either. But he had to admit that it was the safest thing for her, if she wouldn't marry him.

"We could get married," he told her, lowering his voice.

"Can you cook?" Rourke asked. "Besides, I have all my own teeth."

Ted ignored him. He was worried, and it showed. He searched her eyes. "Harris bought a big Bowie at the hardward store yesterday."

"It's not illegal to own a knife," Rourke said.

"Technically it's not, although a Bowie certainly falls under the heading of an illegal weapon if he wears it in town. It has a blade longer than three-and-a-quarter inches. It's the implication of the purchase that concerns me," he added.

Rourke quickly became more somber. "He's making a statement of his intentions," he said.

"That's what I thought," Ted agreed. "And he knows there's not a damned thing I can do about it, unless he carries the weapon blatantly. He's not likely to do that."

Rourke didn't mention that he'd been wearing his own Bowie knife in town. "You could turn your back and I could have a talk with him," Rourke suggested, not completely facetiously.

"He'd have me arrest you, and he'd call his lawyer," was the reply.

"I suppose so."

"Maybe I could visit somebody out of state," Jillian said on a sigh.

"He'd just follow you, and pose a threat to anybody you stayed with," Ted said. "Besides that, you don't know anybody out of state."

"I was only joking," Jillian replied. "I'm not running," she added firmly.

The men looked at her with smiling admiration.

"Foolhardy," Rourke commented.

"Sensible," Ted replied. "Nobody's getting past me in my own town to do her harm."

"I'm not needed at the ranch at night," Rourke said. "I could stay over here."

Ted and Jillian both glared at him.

He threw up his hands. "You people have some incredible hang-ups for twenty-first century human beings!"

"We live in a small town," Jillian pointed out. "I don't want to be talked about. Any more than I already am, I mean," she said miserably. "I guess Harris has convinced half the people here that I'm a heartless flirt who had him arrested because he wanted to marry me."

"Good luck to anybody brain-damaged enough to believe a story like that," Rourke said. "Especially anybody who knows you at all."

"Thanks, Rourke," Jillian replied.

Ted shook his head. "There are people who will believe anything. I'd give real money if I could find a law on the books that I could use to make him leave town."

"Vagrancy would have been a good one until he got that job."

"I agree," Ted said.

"It's not right," Jillian blurted out. "I mean, that somebody can come here, harass me, make my life miserable and just get away with it."

Ted's expression was eloquent. His high cheekbones flushed with impotent bad temper.

"I'm not blaming you," Jillian said at once. "I'm not, Ted. I know there's nothing you can do about it."

"Oh, for the wild old days in Africa," Rourke sighed. "Where we made up the laws as we went along."

"Law is the foundation of any civilization," Ted said firmly.

"True. But law, like anything else, can be abused." Rourke pursed his lips. "Are you staying for supper? I actually brought three steaks."

Jillian frowned. "Three?"

He chuckled. "Let's say I anticipated that we might have company," he said with a wry glance at Ted.

Ted seemed to relax. He gave Jillian an appraising look. "After supper, we might sit on the front porch and do a little target shooting."

She glared at him.

"We could practice with her shotgun," Rourke agreed, adding fuel to the fire.

"I only have two shells," Jillian said curtly.

Rourke reached into a bag he'd placed on a nearby shelf. "I anticipated that, too." He handed the shells to Ted with a grin.

"Double ought buckshot," Ted mused. "We use that in our riot shotguns."

"I know."

"What does that mean?" Jillian wanted to know.

"It's a heavy load, used by law enforcement officers to ensure that criminals who fire on them pay dearly for the privilege," Ted said enigmatically.

"Tears big holes in things, love," Rourke translated.

Ted didn't like the endearment, and his black eyes glittered.

Rourke laughed. "I'll just go turn those steaks."

"Might be safer," Ted agreed.

Rourke left and Ted took Jillian's hand and led her into the living room. He closed the door.

"I don't like him being over here with you alone," he said flatly.

She gave him a hunted look. "Well, I wasn't

exactly overflowing with people trying to protect me from Davy!"

He averted his eyes. "Sorry."

"Why did you get so angry?"

"You were making excuses for him," he said, his voice curt. "Letting him convince you that it was all a mistake. I got access to the court records, Jillian."

She realized what he was saying, and flushed to her hairline.

"Hey," he said softly. "It's not your fault."

"He said I wore suggestive things . . ."

"You never wore suggestive things in your life, and you were fifteen," he muttered. "How would you feel, at your age now, if a fifteen-year-old boy actually flirted with you?"

"I'd tell his mama," she returned.

"Exactly." He waited for that to register.

Her eyes narrowed. "You mean, I didn't have the judgment to involve myself with a man, even one just six years older than me."

"You didn't. And you never wore suggestive things."

"I wasn't allowed, even if I'd wanted to. My uncle was very conservative."

"Harris was a predator. He still is. But in his own mind, he didn't do anything wrong. That's why he's giving you the business. He really feels that he had every right to pursue you. He can't understand why he was arrested for it."

"But that's crazy!"

"No crazier than you second-guessing your own reactions, when you actually had to run to a neighbor's house to save yourself from assault," he pointed out.

She gnawed her lower lip. "I was scared to death." She looked up at him. "Men are so strong," she said. "Even thin men like Davy. I almost didn't get away. And when I did, he went nuts. He was yelling threats all the way to the Peales' house. I really think he would have killed me if Sassy hadn't pulled that shotgun. He might have killed her, too, and it would have been my fault, for running over there for help. But it was the only house close enough."

"I'm sure Sassy never blamed you for that. She's a good person."

"So are you," she commented quietly. "I'm sorry I've been such a trial to you."

His face softened. His black eyes searched hers. "I should have been more understanding." He grimaced. "You don't get how it is, Jake, to go out with a woman you want and be apprehensive about even touching her."

She had a blank look on her face.

"You don't know what I'm talking about, do you?" he asked in a frustrated tone. He moved closer. "Maybe it's time you did."

He curled her into his body with a long, powerful arm and bent his head. He kissed her with soft persuasion at first, then, when she relaxed, his mouth became invasive. He teased her lips apart and nibbled them. He felt her stiffen at first, but after a few seconds, she became more flexible. She stopped resisting and stood very still.

She hadn't known that she could feel such things. Up until now, Ted had been almost teasing when he kissed her. But this time, he wasn't holding anything back. His arm, at her back, arched her up against him. His big hand smoothed up from her waist and brushed lightly at the edges of her small, firm breast.

She really should protest, she told herself. She shouldn't let him do that. But as the kisses grew longer and hungrier, her body began to feel swollen and hot. She ached for more than she was getting, but she didn't understand what she wanted.

Ted felt those vague longings in her and knew how to satisfy them. His mouth ground down onto hers as his fingers began to smooth over the soft mound of flesh, barely touching, kindling hungers that Jillian had never known before.

She gasped when his fingers rubbed over the nipple and it became hard and incredibly sensitive. She tried to draw back, but not with any real enthusiasm.

"Scared?" he whispered against her mouth. "No need. We have a chaperone."

"The door . . . it's closed."

"Yes, thank goodness," he groaned, "because if it wasn't, I wouldn't dare do this."

"This" involved the sudden rise of her shirt and the bra up under her chin and the shocking, delicious, invasion of Ted's warm mouth over her breast.

She shuddered. It was the most intense pleasure she'd ever felt. Her short nails dug into his broad shoulders as she closed her eyes and arched backward to give him even better access to the soft, warm flesh that ached for his tender caress.

She felt his hand cupping her, lifting her, as his mouth opened over the nipple and he took it between his lips and tongue.

Her soft gasp was followed by a harsh, shivering little moan that cost him his control. Not only had it been a long, dry spell, but this woman was the most important person in his life and he wanted her with an obsessive hunger. He hadn't been able to sleep for thinking about how sweet it would be to make love to her. And now she was, despite her hang-ups, not only welcoming his touch, but enjoying it.

"You said you didn't want to marry me," he whispered roughly as his mouth became more demanding.

Her nails dug into his back. "I said a lot of things," she agreed. Her eyes closed as she savored the spicy smell of his cologne, the tenderness of his mouth on forbidden flesh. "I might have even . . . believed them, at the time."

He lifted his head and looked down at her. His expression tautened at the sight of her pretty, firm breasts, and his body clenched. "I took it personally. Like you thought there was something wrong with me."

"Ted, no!" she exclaimed.

He pulled back the hand that was tracing around her nipple.

She bit her lip. "I wasn't saying no to that," she said with hopeless shyness, averting her eyes. "I meant, I don't think there's anything wrong with you . . . !"

She gasped as he responded to the blatant invitation in her voice and teased the hard rise of flesh with his thumb and forefinger.

"You don't?" he whispered, and smiled at her in a way that he never had before.

"Of course not! I was just scared," she managed, because what he was doing was creating sensations in some very private places. "Scared of marriage, I mean."

"Marriage is supposed to be a feast of pleasure for two people who care about each other," he pointed out, watching with delight her fascination with what he was doing to her willing body. He drew in a long breath and bent his head. "I'm beginning to believe it."

He opened his mouth over her soft breast and

drew it inside, suckling it with his lips and his tongue in a slow, easy caress that caused her whole body to clench and shiver. As his ardor increased, he felt with wonder the searching fingers on the buttons of his shirt. They hesitated.

"Men like to be touched, too," he whispered into her ear.

"Oh."

She finished opening the button, a little clumsily, and spread her hands over the thick, curling mass of hair that covered his chest. "Wow," she whispered when sensations rippled through her body and seemed to be echoed coming from his. "You like that?" she asked hesitantly.

"I love it," he gritted.

She smiled with the joy of discovery as she looked up at him, at his mussed hair, his sensuous mouth, his sparkling black eyes. It was new, this shared pleasure. And she'd been so certain that she'd never be able to feel it with him, with anyone.

He bent to her mouth and crushed his lips down over it as his body eased onto hers. She felt the press of his bare chest against her breasts and arched up to increase the contact. Her arms went around him tightly, holding on as the current of passion swept her along.

He eased one long, powerful leg between both of hers and moved against her in a rhythm that drew shudders and soft moans from her throat. She buried her teeth in his shoulder as the sensations began to rise and become obsessive. He must have felt something comparable, because he suddenly pushed down against her with a harsh groan as his control began to slip.

The soft knock on the door came again and again, until it was finally a hammering.

Ted lifted his head, his shocked eyes on Jillian's pretty pink breasts with visible passion marks, her face flushed and rigid with desire, her eyes turbulent as they met his.

"What?" Ted said aloud.

"Steak's ready! Don't let it get cold!" Rourke called, and there were audible footsteps going back down the hall.

With the passion slowly receding, Jillian was disturbed at letting Ted see her like this. Flushed, she fumbled her blouse and bra back on, wincing as the sensitive nipple was brushed by the fabric.

"Sorry," he whispered huskily. "I lost my head."

She managed a shaky smile. "It's okay. I lost mine, too." She looked at him with absolute wonder. "I didn't know it could feel like that," she stammered. "I mean, I never felt like that with anybody. Not that I ever let any man do that . . . !"

He put a long finger over her lips and smiled at her in a way he never had before. "It's okay, Jake."

She was still trying to catch her breath, and not doing a good job of it.

"I think you could say that we're compatible, in that way," he mused, enjoying her reaction to him more than he could find a way to express.

She laughed softly. "Yes, I think you could."

He smiled. "So, suppose we get married. And you can live with me, here on the ranch, and you'll never have to worry about Harris again."

She hesitated, but not for very long. She nodded, slowly. "Okay."

His high cheekbones went a ruddy color. It flattered him that she'd agree after a torrid passionate interlude, when he hadn't been able to persuade her with words.

"Don't get conceited," she said firmly, figuring out his thoughts.

His eyes twinkled. "Not possible."

She laughed. It was as if the world had changed completely in those few minutes. All her hang-ups had gone into eclipse the minute Ted turned the heat up.

"I wondered," he confessed, "if you'd be able to respond to a man after what happened to you."

"I did, too." She moved close to him and put her hands on his chest. "It was one reason I was afraid to let things go, well, very far. I didn't want to lead you on in any way and then pull away and run. I almost did that once."

"Yes," he said.

"If we get married, you'll give me a little time,

won't you?" she asked worriedly. "I mean, I think I can do what you want me to. But it's just getting used to the idea."

Ted, who knew more than she did about women's reactions when passion got really hot, only smiled. "No problem."

She grinned. "Okay, then. Do we get married in the justice of the peace's office . . . ?"

"In a church," he interrupted. "And you have to have a white gown and carry a bouquet. I'll even wear my good suit." He smiled. "I'm only getting married once, you know. We have to do it right."

She loved that attitude. It was what she'd wanted, but she was sensitive about being pushy. "Okay," she said.

"You'll be beautiful in a wedding gown," he murmured, bending to kiss her tenderly. "Not that you aren't beautiful in blue jeans. You are."

"I'm not," she faltered.

"You are to me," he corrected. His black eyes searched hers and he thought about the future, about living with her, about loving her . . . He bent and kissed her hungrily, delighting when she returned the embrace fervently.

"The steak's going to be room temperature in about thirty seconds!" Rourke shouted down the hall.

Ted pulled back, laughing self-consciously. "I guess we could eat steak, since he's been nice enough to cook it," he told her. His eyes glittered. "We can tell him we're engaged before we even start eating."

"Rourke's not interested in me that way," she said easily, smiling. "He's a nice man, but he's just protective of women. It isn't even personal."

Ted had his doubts about that. Jillian underestimated her appeal to men.

"Come on," she said, and slid her little hand into his big one.

That knocked the argument right out of him. It was the first physical move she'd made toward him. Well, not the first, but a big one, just the same. He slid his fingers between hers sensually, and smiled at her.

She smiled back. Her heart was hammering, her senses were alive and tumultuous. It was the beginning of a whole new life. She could hardly wait to marry Ted.

Rourke gave them a knowing smile when he noticed the telltale signs of what they'd been doing. He served up supper.

"This is really good," Ted exclaimed when he took the first bite of his steak.

"I'm a gourmet chef," Rourke replied, surprisingly. "In between dangerous jobs, I used to work in one of the better restaurants in Jo'burg," he said, giving Johannesburg its affectionate abbreviation.

“Wonders will never cease,” Jillian said with a grin. “From steaks to combat.”

“Oh, it was always combat first,” Rourke said easily, “since I was born in Africa.”

“Africa was always a rough venue, from what Cash told me,” Ted said.

Rourke nodded. “We have plenty of factions, all trying to gain control of the disputed African states, although each is a sovereign nation in the Organization of African Unity, which contains fifty-four nations. The wars are always bloody. And there are millions upon millions of displaced persons, trying to survive with their children. A mercenary doesn’t even have to look for work, it’s all around him.” His face hardened. “What’s hardest is what they do to the kids.”

“They must die very young there,” Jillian commented sadly.

“No. They put automatic weapons in their hands when they’re grammar school age, teach them to fire rocket launchers and set explosive charges. They have no sense of what childhood should actually be.”

“Good heavens!” she exclaimed.

“You’ve never traveled, Jake,” Ted said gently. “The world is a lot bigger than Hollister.”

“I guess it is. But I never had the money, even if I’d had the inclination,” she said.

“That’s why I joined the army.” Ted chuckled. “I knew it was the only way I’d get to travel.”

"I wanted to see the world, too." Rourke nodded. "But most of what I've seen of it wouldn't be appropriate for any travel magazine."

"You have a ranch?" Ted asked.

He smiled. "Yes, I do. Luckily it's not in any of the contested areas, so I don't have to worry about politicians seizing power and taking over private land."

"And you run Brahmas," Ted said, shaking his head. "Ugly cattle."

"They're bred to endure the heat and sometimes drought conditions that we have in Africa," Rourke explained. "Our cattle have to be hearty. And some of your American ranchers use them as breeding stock for that very reason."

"I know. I've seen a lot of them down in Texas."

"They don't mind heat and drought, something you can't say for several other breed of cattle," Rourke added.

"I guess," Jillian said.

Rourke finished his steak and took a sip of the strong coffee he'd brewed. "Harris has been frustrated because Jillian got one of the waitresses to start putting cakes out for her in the display case."

"They haven't been selling," Jillian said sadly. "They used to be very popular, and now hardly anybody wants slices of them. I guess Davy has convinced people that they shouldn't eat my cooking because I'm such a bad person."

"Oh, that's not true," Ted said at once. "Don't you know about the contest?"

She frowned. "What contest?"

"You don't read the local paper, do you?" Rourke chided her.

She shook her head. "We already know what's going on, we only read a paper to know who got caught. But I have him," she pointed at Ted, "to tell me that, so why do I need to spend money for a newspaper?"

They both laughed.

"The mayor challenged everyone in Hollister to give up sweets for two weeks. It's a competition between businesses and people who work for them. At the end of the two weeks, everybody gets weighed, and the business with the employees who lost the most weight gets a cash prize, put up by the businesses themselves. The employees get to decide how the money's spent, too, so they can use it for workplace improvements or cash bonuses."

Jillian perked up. "Then it isn't about me!"

"Of course not," Ted chuckled. "I've heard at least two men who eat in that restaurant complain because they couldn't eat those delicious cakes until the contest ended."

"I feel so much better," she said.

"I'm glad," Rourke told her. "But that still doesn't solve your problem. Harris bought a Bowie knife and he doesn't hunt." He let the implication sink in. "He's facing at least ten to fifteen on the charges if he goes back to trial and is convicted again. He's been heard saying that he'll never go back to that hellhole voluntarily. So basically he's got nothing to lose." He glanced at Ted. "You know that already."

Ted nodded. "Yes, I do," he replied. He smiled at Jillian. "Which is why we're getting married Saturday."

She gasped. "Saturday? But there's not enough time . . . !"

"There is. We'll manage. Meanwhile," Ted said, "you're going to take Sassy's invitation seriously and stay out at her ranch until the ceremony. Right?"

She wanted to argue, but both males had set faces and determined expressions. So she sighed and said, "Right."

Chapter 10

Not only did John and Sassy Callister welcome Jillian as a houseguest, Sassy threw herself into wedding preparations and refused to listen to Jillian's protests.

"I've never gotten to plan a wedding, not even my own," Sassy laughed. "John hired a professional to do it for us because so many important people came to the ceremony. So now I'm taking over preparations for yours."

"But I can't afford this store," the younger woman tried to complain. "They don't even put price tags on this stuff!"

Sassy gave her a smile. "John and I agreed that our wedding present to you is going to be the gown and accessories," she said. "So you can hand it down through your family. You might have a daughter who'd love to wear it at her own wedding."

Jillian hadn't thought about that. She became dreamy. A child. A little girl that she could take on walks, cuddle and rock, read stories to. That was a part of marriage she'd never dwelled on before. Now, it was a delightful thought.

"So stop arguing," Sassy said gently, "and start making choices."

Jillian hugged her. "Thanks. For the gown and for letting me stay with you until the wedding."

"This is what friends are for. You'd do it for me in a heartbeat if our situations were reversed."

"Yes, but I could have gotten you killed that night by running to you for help," Jillian said. "It torments me."

"I was perfectly capable of handling Davy Harris. And now I've got John, who can handle anything."

"You're very lucky. He's a good man."

"Yes, he is," Sassy agreed with a smile.

"I've never seen anything as beautiful as these dresses," Jillian began.

"I hear you're getting married Saturday, Jilly," came a cold, taunting voice from behind her.

Both women turned. Davy Harris was watching them, a nasty look on his face.

"Yes, I'm getting married," Jillian told him.

"There was a time when I thought you'd marry me," he said. "I had it all planned, right down to what sort of dress you'd wear and where we'd live. I'd lined up a full-time job with a local rancher. Everything was set." His lips twisted. "Then you had to go and get outraged when I tried to show you how I felt."

"I'll show you how I feel," Sassy said pertly. "Where's my shotgun?"

"Terroristic threats and acts, Mrs. Callister," he shot back. "Suppose I call the news media and tell them that you're threatening me?"

Jillian was horrified.

Sassy just smiled. "Well, wouldn't it be a shame if that same news media suddenly got access to the trial transcripts?" she asked pleasantly.

His face hardened. "You think you're so smart. Women are idiots. My father always said so. My mother was utterly worthless. She couldn't even cook without burning something!"

Jillian stared at him. "That doesn't make a woman worthless."

"She was always nervous," he went on, as if she hadn't spoken. "She called the police once, but my father made sure she never did it again. They put him in prison. I never understood why. She had him locked up. He was right to make her pay for it."

Sassy and Jillian exchanged disturbed looks.

Harris gave Jillian a chilling smile. "He died in prison. But I won't. I'm never going back." He shrugged. "You enjoy thinking about that wedding, Jilly. Because all you're going to get to do is think about it. Have a nice day, now."

He walked out.

The shopping trip was ruined for Jillian. Sassy insisted that they get the gown and the things that went with it, but Jillian was certain that Davy had meant what he said. He was going to try to kill her. Maybe he'd even kill himself, afterward. In his own mind, he was justified. There was no way to reason with such a person, a man who thought that his own mother deserved to die because she'd had his father arrested for apparently greatly abusing her.

"You know, there are scary people in the world," Jillian told Sassy in a subdued tone. "I'll bet if Uncle John had ever really talked to Davy, he'd never have let him in the front door in the first place. He's mentally disturbed, and it isn't apparent until he starts talking about himself."

"I noticed that," Sassy replied. She drew in a long breath. "I'm glad we have Rourke."

Jillian frowned. "Where is he?"

"Watching us. If Harris had made a threatening move, he'd already be in jail, probably after a trip to the emergency room. I've never seen Rourke mad, but John says it's something you don't want to experience."

"I got that impression." She laughed. "He cooked steaks for Ted and me."

"I heard about that," the other woman said in an amused tone. "Ted was jealous, was he?"

"Very. But after he realized that Rourke was just being friendly and protective, his attitude changed. Apparently he knows a police chief in Texas that Ted met at a workshop back east."

"Rourke does get around." She glanced at Jillian. "He acts like a perpetual clown, but if you see him when he thinks he's alone, it's all an act. He's a very somber, sad person. I think he's had some rough knocks."

"He doesn't talk about them much. Just about his ranch."

"He doesn't talk about K.C. Kantor, either," Sassy replied. "But there's some sound gossip about the fact that Rourke's mother was once very close to the man."

"From what everybody says about that Kantor man, he isn't the sort to have kids."

"That's what I thought. But a man can get into a situation where he doesn't think with his mind," Sassy chuckled. "And when people get careless, they have kids."

"I'd be proud of Rourke, if I was his father."

"You're the wrong age and gender," Sassy said, tongue in cheek.

"Oh, you know what I mean. He's a good person."

"He is," Sassy said as she pulled up in front of the ranch house. "I'm glad John hired him. At least we don't have to worry about being assassinated on the way to town!"

"Amen," Jillian sighed.

John Callister was an easygoing, friendly man. He didn't seem at all like a millionaire, or at least, Jillian's vision of one. He treated her as he would a little sister, and was happy to have her around.

Jillian also liked Sassy's mother, who was in poor health, and her adopted sister, Selene, who was a whiz at math and science in grammar school. John took care of them, just as he took care of Sassy.

But the easygoing personality went into eclipse when he heard that Davy Harris had followed them into the dress shop in Billings.

"The man is dangerous," he said as they ate an early supper with Rourke.

"He is," Rourke agreed. "He shouldn't be walking around loose in the first place. What the hell is wrong with the criminal justice system in this country?"

John gave him a droll look. "It's better than the old vigilante system of the distant past," he pointed out. "And it usually works."

"Not with Harris," Rourke replied, his jaw set as he munched on a chef's salad. "He can put on a good act for a while, but he can't keep it up. He starts talking, and you see the lunacy underneath the appearance of sanity."

"Disturbed people often don't know they're disturbed," Sassy said.

"That's usually the case, I'm sad to say," Rourke added. "People like Harris always think they're being persecuted."

"I knew a guy once who was sure the government sent invisible spies to watch him," John mused. "He could see them, but nobody else could. He worked for us one summer on the ranch back home. Gil and I put up with him because he was the best horse wrangler we'd ever had. But that was a mistake."

"How so?" Rourke asked.

"Well, he had this dog. It was vicious and he refused to get rid of it. One day it came right up on the porch and threatened Gil's little girls. Gil punched him and fired him. Then he started cutting fences and killing cattle. At the last, he tried to kill us. He ended up in prison, too."

"Good heavens!" Jillian said. "No wonder you hired a bodyguard for Sassy."

"Exactly," John replied tersely. He didn't mention that Sassy had been the victim of a predator herself, in the feed store where she was working when they met. That man was serving time now.

His eyes lingered on Sassy with warm affection. "Nobody's hurting my best girl. Or her best friend," he declared with a grin at Jillian.

"Not while I'm on the job," Rourke added, chuckling. "You could marry me, you know," he told Jillian. "I really do have most of my own teeth left, and I can cook. Your fiancé can't boil water, I hear."

"That's true," Jillian said, smiling. "But I've known him most of my life, and we think the same way about most things. We'll have a good marriage." She was sure of that. Ted would be gentle, and patient, and he'd rid her of the distaste Davy had left in her about physical relationships. She'd never been more certain of anything.

"Well, it's a great shame," Rourke said with a theatrical sigh. "I'll have to go back home to my ugly cattle and live in squalor because nobody wants to take care of me."

"You'll find some lovely girl who will be happy living on a small farm in Africa," Jillian assured him.

John almost choked on his coffee.

Rourke gave him a cold glare.

"What is wrong with you?" Sassy asked her husband.

He wiped his mouth, still stifling laughter. "Private joke," he said, sharing a look with Rourke, who sighed and shrugged.

"But it had better be somebody who can dress bullet wounds," John added with a twinkle in his eyes as he glanced at the other man.

"I only get shot occasionally," Rourke assured him. "And I usually duck in time."

"That's true," John agreed, forking another piece of steak into his mouth. "He only has one head wound, and it doesn't seem to have affected his thinking processes." He didn't mention the lost eye, because Rourke was sensitive about it.

"That was a scalp wound," Rourke replied, touching a faint scar above his temple. He glared at the other man from a pale brown eye. "And not from a bullet. It was from a knife."

"Poor thing," Jillian murmured.

John choked on his steak.

"Will you stop?" Rourke muttered.

"Sorry." John coughed. He sipped coffee.

Jillian wished she knew what they were talking about. But it was really none of her business, and she had other worries.

The wedding gown was exquisite. She couldn't stop looking at it. She hung it on the door in the guest bedroom and sighed over it at every opportunity.

Ted came by to visit frequently and they took long walks in the woods, to talk and to indulge in a favorite of dating couples, the hot physical interludes that grew in intensity by the day.

He held her hand and walked with her down a long path through the snow, his fingers warm and strong in hers.

"I can't stand it if I go a whole day without seeing you," he said out of the blue.

She stopped walking and looked up at him with pure wonder. "Really?"

He pulled her into his arms. "Really." He bent and kissed her slowly, feeling her respond, feeling her warm lips open and move tenderly. She reached her arms up around his neck as if it was the most natural thing in the world. He smiled against her lips. It was a delightful surprise, her easy response to him.

"Maybe I can get used to Sammy following me around, and you can get used to me shooting targets off the front porch," he teased.

She grinned. "Maybe you can teach me to shoot, too."

He looked shocked. "I can?"

"We should share some interests," she said wisely. "You always go to that shooting range and practice. I could go with you sometimes."

He was surprised and couldn't hide it.

She toyed with a shirt button. "I don't like being away from you, either, Ted," she confessed and flushed a little. "It's so sweet . . ."

He pulled her close. One lean hand swept down her back, riveting her to his powerful body. "Sweeter than honey," he managed before he kissed her.

His hand pushed her hips against the sudden hardness of his own, eliciting a tiny sound from her throat. But it wasn't protest. If anything, she moved closer.

He groaned out loud and ground her hips into his.

"I can't wait until Saturday," he said in a husky tone, easing his hands under Jillian's blouse, under the bra to caress her soft breasts. "I'm dying!"

"So am I," she whispered shakily. "Oh, Ted!" she gasped when he pulled the garments out of his way and covered her breast with his mouth. It was so sweet. Too sweet for words!

He didn't realize what he was doing until they were lying on the cold ground, in the snow, while he kissed her until she was breathless.

She was shaking when he lifted his head, but not from cold or fear. Her eyes held the same frustrated desire that his held.

"I want to, so much!" she whispered.

"So do I," he replied.

For one long instant, they clung together on the hard ground, with snow making damp splotches all down Jillian's back and legs, while they both fought for control.

Ted clenched his hands beside her head and closed his eyes as he rested his forehead against hers. He was rigid, helplessly aroused and unable to hide it.

She smoothed back his black hair and pressed soft, undemanding little kisses all over his taut face, finally against the closed eyelids and short thick black lashes.

"It's all right," she whispered. "It's all right."

He was amazed at the effect those words, and the caresses, had on him. They eased the torment. They calmed him, in the sweetest way he'd ever imagined. He smiled against her soft throat.

"Learning how to tame the beast, aren't you?" he whispered in a teasing tone.

She looked up at him with soft, loving eyes. "How to calm him down, anyway," she said with a little laugh. "I think marriage is going to be an adventure."

"So do I."

He stood and tugged her up, too, helping to rearrange her disheveled clothing. He grinned at her. "We both love maps and the tango. We'll go dancing every week."

Her eyes brightened. "I'd like that."

He enveloped her against him and stood holding her, quietly, in the silence of the snow-covered woods. "Heaven," he whispered, "must be very like this."

She smiled, hugging him. "I could die of happiness."

His heart jumped. "So could I, sweetheart."

The endearment made her own heart jump. She'd never been so happy in her life.

"Saturday can't come soon enough for me," he murmured.

"Or for me. Ted, Sassy bought me the most beautiful wedding gown. I know you aren't supposed to see it before the ceremony, but I just have to show it to you."

He drew back, smiling. "I'd like that."

They walked hand in hand back to the ranch house, easy and content with each other in a way they'd never been before. They looked as if they'd always been together, and always would be.

Sassy, busy in the kitchen with the cook, grinned at them. "Staying for lunch, Ted? We're having chili and Mexican corn bread."

"I'd love to, if you have enough to share."

"Plenty."

"Then, thanks, I will. Jillian wants me to see the wedding gown."

"Bad luck," Sassy teased.

"We make our own luck, don't we, honey?" he asked Jillian in a husky, loving tone.

She blushed at the second endearment in very few minutes and squeezed his hand. "Yes, we do."

She opened her bedroom door and gasped, turning pale. There, on the floor, were the remains of her wedding gown, her beautiful dress. It had been slashed to pieces.

"Stop right there," Ted said curtly, his arm preventing Jillian from entering the room. "This is now a crime scene. I'll get the sheriff's department's investigator out here right now, and the state crime-lab techs. I know who did this. I only want enough proof to have him arrested!"

Jillian wrapped her arms around her chest and shivered. Davy had come right into the house and nobody knew. Not even Rourke. It was chilling. Sassy, arriving late, took in the scene with a quick glance and hugged Jillian.

"It will be all right," she promised. But her own eyes were troubled. It was scary that he'd come into the house without being seen.

Rourke, when he realized what had happened, was livid. "That polecat!" he snarled. "Right under my bloody nose, and me like a raw recruit with no clue he was on the place! That won't happen again! I'm calling in markers. I'll have this place like a fortress before Saturday!"

Nobody argued with him. The situation had become a tragedy in the making. They'd all underestimated Davy Harris's wilderness skills, which were apparently quite formidable.

"He was a hunter," Jillian recalled. "He showed me how to track deer when he first started working with Uncle John, before he got to be a problem. He could walk so nobody heard a step. I'd forgotten that."

"I can ghost-walk myself," Rourke assured her.

"He used to set bear traps," Jillian blurted out, and reddened when everybody looked at her. "He said it was to catch a wolf that had been preying on the calves, but Uncle John said there was a dog caught in it . . ." She felt sick. "I'd forgotten that."

The men looked at each other. A bear trap could be used for many things, including catching unsuspecting people.

Jillian stared at Ted with horror. "Ted, he wouldn't use that on Sammy, would he?" she asked fearfully. Davy knew how much she loved her calf.

"No," he assured her with a comforting arm around her shoulders as he lied. "He wouldn't."

Rourke left the room for a few minutes. He came back, grim-faced. "We're going to have a lot of company very soon. All we need is proof that he was here, and he won't be a problem again."

• • •

Which would have been wonderful. Except that there wasn't a footprint in the dirt, a fingerprint, or any trace evidence whatsoever that Davy Harris had been near the Callister home. The technicians with all their tools couldn't find one speck of proof.

"So much for Locard's Exchange Principle," Ted said grimly, and then had to explain what it meant to Jillian. "A French criminalist named Edmond Locard noted that when a crime is committed, the perpetrator both carries away and leaves behind trace evidence."

"But Davy didn't," she said sadly.

"He's either very good or very lucky," Ted muttered. He slid a protective arm around Jillian. "And it won't save him. He's the only person in town who had a motive for doing this. It's just a matter of proving it."

She laughed hollowly. "Maybe you could check his new Bowie knife to see if it's got pieces of white lace sticking to it," she said, trying to make the best of a bad situation.

But he didn't laugh. He was thoughtful. "That might not be such a bad idea," he murmured. "All I'd need is probable cause, if I can convince a judge to issue a search warrant on the basis of it." He pursed his lips and narrowed his eyes, nodding to himself. "And that's just what I'm going to do. Stick close to the house today, okay?"

"Okay."

He kissed her and left.

But Ted came back a few hours later and stuck to her like glue. She noticed that he was suddenly visible near her, everywhere she went around the house and the barn. It was just after he'd received a phone call, to which nobody was privy.

"What's going on?" Jillian asked him bluntly.

He smiled, his usual easygoing self, as he walked beside her with his hands deep in the pockets of his khaki slacks. "What would be going on?"

"You're usually at work during the day, Ted," she murmured dryly.

He grinned at her. "Maybe I can't stay away from you, even on a workday," he teased.

She stopped and turned to him, frowning. "That's not an answer and you know . . . !"

She gasped as he suddenly whirled, pushing her to the ground as he drew his pistol and fired into a clump of snow-covered undergrowth near the house. Even as he fired, she felt a sting in her arm and then heard a sound like a high-pitched crack of thunder.

That sound was followed by the equally loud rapid fire of a .45 automatic above her. She heard the bullets as they connected with tree trunks in the distance.

"You okay?" he asked urgently.

"I think so."

He stopped firing, and eased up to his feet, standing very still with his head cocked, listening. Far in the distance was the sound of a vehicle door closing, then an engine starting. He whipped out his cell phone and made a call. He gave a quick explanation, a quicker description of the direction of travel of the vehicle and assurances that the intended victim was all right. He put up the cell phone and knelt beside a shaken Jillian.

There was blood on her arm. The sleeve of her gray sweatshirt was ripped. She looked at it with growing sensation. It stung.

"What in the world?" she stammered.

"You've been hit, sweetheart," he said curtly. "That's a gunshot wound. I didn't want to tell you, but one of my investigators learned that Harris bought a high-powered rifle with a telescopic sight this morning, after I had his rented room tossed for evidence."

"He's a convicted felon, nobody could have sold him a gun at all . . . !" she burst out.

"There are places in any town, even small ones, where people can buy weapons under the table." His face was hard as stone. "I don't know who sold it to him, but you'd better believe that I'm going to find out. And God help whoever did, when I catch up to him!"

She was still trying to wrap her mind around the fact that she'd been shot. Rourke, who'd been at the other end of the property, came screeching up in a ranch Jeep and jumped out, wincing when he saw the blood on Jillian's arm.

"I spotted him, I was tracking him, when I heard the gunshot. God, I'm sorry!" he exclaimed. "I should have been quicker. Do you think you hit him?" he asked Ted.

"I'm not sure. Maybe." He helped Jillian up. "I'll get you to a doctor." He glanced at Rourke. "I called the sheriff to bring his dogs and his best investigator out here," he added. "They may need some help. I told the sheriff you'd been on the case, working for the Callisters."

Rourke's pale brown eye narrowed. He looked far different from the man Jillian had come to know as her easygoing friend. "I let him get onto the property, and I'm sorry. But I can damned sure track him."

"None of us could have expected what happened here," Ted said reassuringly, and put a kindly hand on the other man's shoulder. "She'll be okay. Sheriff's department investigator is on his way out here. I gave the sheriff's investigator your cell phone number," Ted added.

Rourke nodded. He winced at Jillian's face. "I'm sorry," he said curtly.

She smiled, holding her arm. "It's okay, Rourke."

"I didn't realize he was on the place, either, until I heard the gunshots," Ted said.

"Not the first time you've been shot at, I gather?" she asked with black humor.

"Not at all. You usually feel the bullet before you hear the sound," he added solemnly.

"And that's a fact," Rourke added with faint humor.

"Let's go," Ted said gently.

She let him put her into the patrol car. She was feeling sick, and she was in some pain. "It didn't hurt at first," she said. "I didn't even realize I was shot. Oh, Ted, I'm sorry, you have to wait . . . !" She opened the door and threw up, then she cried with embarrassment.

He handed her a clean white handkerchief, put her back in the car, and broke speed limits getting her to the emergency room.

"It's never like that on television," she said drowsily, when she'd been treated and was in a semi-private room for the night. They'd given her something for pain, as well. It was making her sleepy.

"What isn't, sweetheart?"

She smiled at the endearment as he leaned over her, gently touching her face. "People getting shot. They don't throw up."

"That's not real life, either," he reminded her.

She was worried, but not only for herself.

"What is it?" he asked gently.

"Sammy," she murmured. "I know, it's stupid to

be worried about a calf, but if he can't get to me, he might try to hurt something I love." She searched his eyes. "You watch out, too."

His dark eyes twinkled. "Because you love me?" he drawled.

She only nodded, her face solemn. "More than anyone in the world."

There was a flush on his high cheekbones. He cupped her head in his big hands and kissed her with blatant possession. "That goes double for me," he whispered against her lips.

She searched his eyes with fascination. "It does?"

"Why in the world do you think I'd want to marry you if I didn't love you?" he asked reasonably. "No parcel of land is worth that sort of sacrifice."

"You never said," she stammered.

"Neither did you," he pointed out, chuckling.

She laid her hand against his shoulder. "I didn't want to say it first."

He kissed her nose. "But you did."

She sighed and smiled. "Yes. I did."

For one long moment, they were silent together, savoring the newness of an emotion neither had realized was so intense.

Finally he lifted his head. "I don't want to leave you, but we've got a lot of work to do and not a lot of time to do it."

She nodded. "You be careful."

"I will."

"Ted, could you check on Sammy?" she asked worriedly.

"Yes. I'll make sure she's okay."

She smiled. "Thanks."

"No problem."

Sassy came and took her back to the Callister ranch as soon as the doctor released her.

"I still think they should have kept you overnight," Sassy muttered.

"They tried to, but I refused," Jillian said drowsily. "I don't like being in hospitals. Have you heard anything more?"

"About Harris?" Sassy shook her head. "I know they've got dogs in the woods, hunting him. But if he's a good woodsman, he'll know how to cover his trail."

"He talked about that once," Jillian recalled. "He said there were ways to cover up a scent trail so a dog couldn't track people. Funny, I never wondered why he'd know such a thing."

"I'm sorry he does," Sassy replied. "If he didn't have those skills, he'd be a lot easier to find."

"I guess so."

"I've got a surprise for you," Sassy said when they walked into the house. She smiled mysteriously as she led Jillian down the hall to the guest bedroom she'd been occupying.

"What is it?" Jillian asked.

Sassy opened the door. There, hanging on the closet door, was a duplicate of the beautiful wedding gown that Sassy had chosen, right down to the embroidery.

"They only had two of that model. The other was in a store in Los Angeles. I had them overnight it," Sassy chuckled. "Nothing is going to stop this wedding!"

Jillian burst into tears. She hugged Sassy, as close as her wounded arm would permit. "Thank you!"

"It's little enough to do. I'm sorry the other one was ruined. We're just lucky that there was a second one in your size."

Jillian fingered the exquisite lace. "It is the most beautiful gown I'd ever seen. I'll never be able to thank you enough, Sassy."

The other woman was solemn. "We don't talk about it, but I'm sure you know that I had a similar experience, with my former boss at the feed store where I worked just before I married John. I was older than you were, and it wasn't quite as traumatic as yours, but I know how it feels to be assaulted." She sighed. "Funny thing, I had no idea when you came running up to the door with Harris a step behind you that I'd ever face the same situation in my own life."

"I'm sorry."

"Yes, so am I. There are bad men in the world.

But there are good ones, too," Sassy reminded her. "I'm married to one of them, and you're about to marry another one."

"If Davy doesn't find some horrible new way to stop it," Jillian said with real concern in her voice.

"He won't," Sassy said firmly. "There are too many people in uniforms running around here for him to take that sort of a chance."

She bit her lower lip. "Ted was going to see about Sammy. I don't know if Harris might try to hurt her, to get back at me."

"He won't have the chance," Sassy said. "John and two of our hands took a cattle trailer over to your house a few minutes before I left to pick you up at the hospital. They're bringing her over here, and she'll stay in our barn. We have a man full-time who does nothing but look after our prize bulls who live in it."

"You've done so much for me," Jillian said, fighting tears.

"You'd do it for me," was the other woman's warm reply. "Now stop worrying. You have two days to get well enough to walk down the aisle."

"Maybe we should postpone it," she began.

"Not a chance," Sassy replied. "We'll have you back on your feet by then if we have to fly in specialists!" And she meant it.

Chapter 11

Jillian carried a small bouquet of white and pale pink roses as she walked down the aisle of the small country church toward Ted, who was waiting at the altar. Her arm was sore and throbbing a little, and she was still worried about whether or not Davy Harris might try to shoot one of them through the window. But none of her concerns showed in her radiant expression as she took her place beside Ted.

The minister read the marriage ceremony. Jillian repeated the words. Ted repeated them. He slid a plain gold band onto her finger. She slid one onto his. They looked at each other with wonder and finally shared a kiss so tender that she knew she'd remember it all her life.

They held hands walking back down the aisle, laughing, as they were showered with rose petals by two little girls who were the daughters of one of Ted's police officers.

"Okay, now, stand right here while we get the photos," Sassy said, stage-managing them in the reception hall where food and punch were spread out on pristine white linen tablecloths with crystal and china to contain the feast. She'd hired a professional photographer to record the event, over Jillian's protests, as part of the Callisters' wedding gift to them.

Jillian felt regal in her beautiful gown. The night before, she'd gone out to the barn with Ted to make sure little Sammy was settled in a stall. It was silly to be worried about an animal, but she'd been a big part of Jillian's life since she was first born, to a cow that was killed by a freak lightning strike the next day. Jillian had taken the tiny calf to the house and kept her on old blankets on the back porch and fed her around the clock to keep her alive.

That closeness had amused Ted, especially since the calf followed Jillian everywhere she went and even, on occasion, tried to go in the house with her. He supposed he was lucky that they didn't make calf diapers, he'd teased, or Jillian would give the animal a bedroom.

"Did anybody check to see if I left my jacket down that trail where I took Sammy for her walks?" Jillian asked suddenly. "The buckskin one, with the embroidery. It hasn't rained, but if it does, it will be soaked. I forgot all about it when I came to stay with Sassy."

"I'll look for it later," Ted told her, nuzzling her nose with his. "When we go home."

"Home." She sighed and closed her eyes. "I forgot. We'll live together now."

"Yes, we will." He touched her face. "Maybe not as closely as I'd like for a few more days," he teased deeply and chuckled when she flushed. "That arm is going to take some healing."

"I never realized that a flesh wound could cause so much trouble," she told him.

"At least it was just a flesh wound," he said grimly. "Damned if I can figure out why we can't find that polecat," he muttered, borrowing Rourke's favorite term. "We've had men scouring the countryside for him."

"Maybe he got scared and left town," she said hopefully.

"We found his truck deserted, about halfway between the Callisters' ranch and ours," he said. "Dogs lost his trail when it went off the road." He frowned. "One of our trackers said that his footprints changed from one side of the truck to the other, as if he was carrying something."

"Maybe a suitcase?" she wondered.

He shook his head. "We checked the bus station and we had the sheriff's department send cars all over the back roads. He just vanished into thin air."

"I'm not sorry," she said heavily. "But I'd like to know that he wasn't coming back."

"So would I." He bent and kissed her. "We'll manage," he added. "Whatever happens, we'll manage."

She smiled up at him warmly. "Yes. We will."

They settled down into married life. Ted had honestly hoped to wait a day or so until her arm was a little less sore.

But that night while they were watching a movie on television, he kissed her and she kissed him back. Then they got into a more comfortable position on the sofa. Very soon, pieces of clothing came off and were discarded on the floor. And then, skin against skin, they learned each other in ways they never had before.

Just for a minute, it was uncomfortable. He felt her stiffen and his mouth brushed tenderly over her closed eyelids. "Easy," he whispered. "Try to relax. Move with me. Move with me, sweetheart . . . yes!"

And then it was all heat and urgency and explosions of sensation like nothing she'd ever felt in her life. She dug her nails into his hips and moaned harshly as the hard, fierce thrust of his body lifted her to elevations of pleasure that built on each other until she was afraid that she might die trying to survive them.

"Yes," he groaned, and he bruised her thighs with his fingers as he strained to get even closer to her when the pleasure burst and shuddered into ecstacy.

She cried out. Her whole body felt on fire. She moved with him, her own hips arching up in one last surge of strength before the world dissolved into sweet madness.

She was throbbing all over, like her sore arm that she hadn't even noticed until now. She shivered under the weight of Ted's body.

"I was going to wait," he managed in a husky whisper.

"What in the world for?" she laughed. "It's just a sore arm." Her eyes met his with shy delight.

He lifted an eyebrow rakishly. "Is anything else sore?" he asked.

She grinned. "No."

He pursed his lips. "Well, in that case," he whispered, and began to move.

She clutched at him and gasped with pure delight.

He only laughed.

Much later, they curled up together in bed, exhausted and happy. They slept until late the next morning, missing church and a telephone call from the sheriff, Larry Kane.

"Better call me as soon as you get this," Larry said grimly on the message. "It's urgent."

Ted exchanged a concerned glance with Jillian as he picked up his cell phone and returned the call.

"Graves," he said into the phone. "What's up?"

There was a pause while he listened. He scowled. "What?" he exclaimed.

"What is it?" Jillian was mouthing at him.

He held up a hand and sighed heavily. "How long ago?"

He nodded. "Well, it's a pity, in a way. But it's ironic, you have to admit. Yes. Yes. I'll tell her. Thanks, Larry."

He snapped the phone shut. "They found Davy Harris this morning."

"Where is he?" she asked, gnawing her lip.

"They've taken him to the state crime lab."

She blinked. "I thought they only took dead people . . . Oh, dear. He's dead?"

He nodded. "They found him with his leg caught in a bear trap. He'd apparently been trying to set it on the ranch, down that trail where you always walk with Sammy, through the trees where it's hard to see the ground."

"Good Lord!" she exclaimed, and the possibilities created nightmares in her mind.

"He'd locked the trap into place with a log chain, around a tree, and padlocked it in place. Sheriff thinks he lost the key somewhere. He couldn't get the chain loose or free himself from the trap. He bled to death."

She felt sick all over. She pressed into Ted's arms and held on tight. "What a horrible way to go."

"Yes, well, just remember that it was how he planned for Sammy to go," he said, without mentioning that Harris may well have planned to catch Jillian in it.

"His sister will sue us all for wrongful death and say we killed him," Jillian said miserably, remembering the woman's fury when her brother was first arrested.

"His sister died two years ago," he replied. "Of a drug overdose. A truly troubled family."

"When did you find that out?" she wondered.

"Yesterday," he said. "I didn't want to spend our wedding day talking about Harris, but I did wonder if he might run to his sister for protection. So I had an investigator try to find her."

"A sad end," she said.

"Yes. But fortunately, not yours," he replied. He held her close, glad that it was over, finally.

She sighed. "Not mine," she agreed.

Rourke left three days later to go back to Africa. He'd meant to leave sooner, but Sassy and John wanted to show him around Montana first, despite the thick snow that was falling in abundance now.

"I've taken movies of the snow to show back home," he mentioned as he said his farewells to Jillian and Ted while a ranch hand waited in the truck to drive him to the airport in Billings. "We don't get a lot of snow in Kenya," he added, tongue in cheek.

"Thanks for helping keep me alive," Jillian told him.

"My pleasure," he replied, and smiled.

Ted shook hands with him. "If you want to learn how to fish for trout, come back in the spring when the snows melt and we'll spend the day on the river."

"I might take you up on that," Rourke said.

They watched him drive away.

Jillian slid her arm around Ted's waist. "You coming home for lunch?" she asked as they walked to his patrol car.

"Thought I might." He gave her a wicked grin. "You going to fix food or are we going to spend my lunch hour in the usual way?"

She pursed her lips. "Oh, I could make sandwiches."

"You could pack them in a plastic bag," he added, "and I could take them back to work with me."

She flushed and laughed. "Of course. We wouldn't want to waste your lunch hour by eating."

He bent and kissed her with barely restrained hunger. "Absolutely not! See you about noon."

She kissed him back. "I'll be here."

He drove off, throwing up a hand as he went down the driveway. She watched him go and thought how far she'd come from the scared teenager that Davy Harris had intimidated so many years before. She had a good marriage and her life was happier than ever before. She still had her morning job at the local restaurant. She liked the little bit of independence it gave her, and they could use the extra money. Ted wasn't likely to get rich working as a police chief.

On the other hand, their lack of material wealth only brought them closer together and made their shared lives better.

She sighed as she turned back toward the house, her eyes full of dreams. Snow was just beginning to fall again, like a burst of glorious white feathers around her head. Winter was beautiful. Like her life.

DIANA PALMER has a gift for telling the most sensual tales with charm and humor. With more than 40 million copies of her books in print, Diana Palmer is one of North America's most beloved authors and considered one of the top ten romance authors in the United States.

Diana's hobbies include gardening, archaeology, anthropology, art, astronomy and music. She has been married to James Kyle for over thirty-five years. They have one son, Blayne, who is married to the former Christina Clayton, and a granddaughter, Selena Marie.

Center Point Publishing
600 Brooks Road ● PO Box 1
Thorndike ME 04986-0001 USA

(207) 568-3717

US & Canada:
1 800 929-9108
www.centerpointlargeprint.com